"Guard! Arrest this man!"

Carter silenced the officer with a quick thrust to the heart. He withdrew Hugo and turned to the bike, but it was demolished by a stream of 7.62mm slugs from a submachine gun. The fuel tank blew, throwing Carter to the road. He scrambled up, unslung his Kalashnikov and got off a three-round burst in the general direction of the unseen enemy.

No one fired again, but Carter realized he was now extremely vulnerable in the street. He ran toward a group of trees, slid behind one, and watched the area around the burning bike.

Carter heard the snapping of a twig behind him. He started to turn, and something crashed into the back of his head. The pain lasted only a second or two as everything changed from spots of light to black.

"So the killer of my men joins us at last," a voice spoke, coldly...

NICK CARTER IS IT!

"Nick Cartér out-Bonds James Bond."
                        —*Buffalo Evening News*

"Nick Carter is America's #1 espionage agent."
                        —*Variety*

"Nick Carter is razor-sharp suspense."
                        —*King Features*

"Nick Carter has attracted an army of addicted readers
. . . the books are fast, have plenty of action and just the
right degree of sex . . . Nick Carter is the American
James Bond, suave, sophisticated, a killer with both the
ladies and the enemy."
                        —*The New York Times*

FROM THE NICK CARTER
KILLMASTER SERIES

BLACK SEA BLOODBATH

KILL MASTER

NICK CARTER

JOVE BOOKS, NEW YORK

"Nick Carter" is a registered trademark of
The Condé Nast Publications, Inc.,
registered in the United States Patent Office.

KILLMASTER #244: BLACK SEA BLOODBATH

A Jove Book / published by arrangement with
The Condé Nast Publications, Inc.

PRINTING HISTORY
Jove edition / December 1988

ISBN: 0-515-09846-9

Jove Books are published by The Berkley Publishing Group,
200 Madison Avenue, New York, New York 10016.
The name "JOVE" and the "J" logo
are trademarks belonging to Jove Publications, Inc.

PRINTED IN THE UNITED STATES OF AMERICA

10 9 8 7 6 5 4 3 2 1

ONE

The black Zil limousine moved around Red Square at a leisurely pace, its driver enjoying the sweet smell of success. A farmer from Georgia, he had lived the first third of his life in obscurity until his boyhood friend Mikhail Stepanovich Nesterov became party chief at Sukhumi. Miracle of miracles, he was given driving lessons, dressed in a fine uniform, and had driven for the great man ever since.

Nesterov sat in the back enjoying the view as much as his driver. It had been a long struggle to get to the top. He'd started by running errands for the party chief at Sukhumi and had finally reached the exalted position as a member of the Politburo. Nesterov had worked hard, had always been available day and night. It didn't matter that he was not the greatest brain coming out of Georgia. It mattered that he was willing, loyal, and most of all, a close friend of the General Secretary, Serge Federovich Morozov.

Morozov had many things in common with Nesterov. He had been born in Sukhumi. At one time he had been

1

party chief of their district. He too had been willing and loyal. But the similarity stopped there. Morozov was brilliant. He was a politician who could bend minds to his will. Since his elevation to the highest post in the land four years ago, he had consolidated his position in every field of power in the hierarchy of Soviet politics.

Sitting in the limousine as it passed through the massive red brick Spassky Tower, the largest of the towers guarding the entrance to the Kremlin, Nesterov was impressed with the two-hundred-foot-high structure and the sound of the massive bells as they chimed the half hour above his head.

Nesterov was a fat man. In the early years he had been a big man who could not indulge himself. Now he was gross, a man of no great accomplishment, a man of power who happened to have the right friends, a man who could now enjoy the best that Moscow's caterers had to offer. His clothes and the inside of the limousine always smelled of the best Cuban cigars. He had fallen in with the new fad of wearing cologne, but as with everything he touched, he overdid it. He wore the finest imitation Savile Row suits the tailors of Moscow could provide.

Regardless of the attention lavished on him by the merchants of the capital, he still looked like an old bull, smelled like a musky boudoir, and moved on his ponderous shanks like an elephant from the Moscow circus.

The Zil came to a smooth stop at a nondescript stone building in the heart of the Kremlin. The door was opened by one of the uniformed guards who saluted as the huge man pulled himself from the car. A small cloud of smoke followed him as he lumbered up the four stairs to the oak doors and inside where he was greeted by another Georgian, a man of small intellect who could open doors and take coats without fault.

"The General Secretary is waiting in the study, comrade," the simple-looking Georgian said.

"Thank you, Dmitri. What is his mood?" Nesterov asked.

"He sits and thinks as usual," the retainer said. "But he eats and drinks without throwing anything at us today. It is a good day."

Guards stood unobtrusively at strategic points throughout the house. They didn't salute or acknowledge the VIP but stood like statues, only their eyes moving, constantly on the alert. Two attempts had been made on the General Secretary's life inside this very building in the past three years. And Morozov had threatened that if it happened again, he'd have all of the guards castrated and sent to the labor camps.

Nesterov entered the General Secretary's favorite study. Its high ceiling reminded him of a cathedral. The walls were of square panels, all of the finest Ukrainian oak. Old masters, taken from public galleries, hung under subtle lighting. Sculptures and tapestries were placed to advantage, lit by ceiling spots. It was not a place any member of the Politburo would like the man on the street to see. Luxury was not for viewing. But it was a way of life for Serge Federovich Morozov.

The great man sat in a wing chair surrounded on three sides by a U-shaped table he'd ordered designed for his everyday use. This was where he could usually be found for as long as eighteen hours a day. He was a modern man, surrounded by monitors that could show him every corner of the Soviet Union and, by satellite, every corner of the world.

When Nesterov entered, the monitors were recessed within the desk and the leader sat slumped in his chair, looking at the ceiling, deep in thought.

Morozov was a handsome man by any standard. He managed to keep himself at about 220 pounds, which suited his six-feet-one frame ideally. He had a high forehead and strong jaw, and his best features were his eyes that seemed to penetrate to the very soul of his visitors.

"Misha," he said, a smile spreading across his face. "I was pleased to hear you were in Moscow. It is time for one of our talks."

Nesterov had no illusions about his role. While he knew he was only a sounding board, he took pride in the fact that the General Secretary chose him for the role. His objectives were unlike his grasping peers. He wanted only the status quo. His influence had already taken him far beyond his capabilities.

"It is my pleasure, Serge Federovich," he said, lowering himself ponderously into a second massive wing chair. One at a time, Nesterov pulled his feet to rest on a nearby footstool, using both hands, then sat back, winded.

"You should lose some weight, old friend," the General Secretary chided. "Fat men die young."

Nesterov reached for the vodka bottle without asking and poured a tumbler for himself. "Tomorrow," he chuckled. "Perhaps tomorrow."

Both men raised their glasses and drained them.

"How is our project going back home?" the General Secretary asked.

When he had come to power, the first thing Morozov had ordered was a massive change of administration in the Ministry of National Science. The old Academy of Science was bulging at the seams. It needed extensive expansion, considering the rapid developments in fields such as laser technology and artificial intelligence.

At the same time, Morozov wanted to put his mark on the new regime, to make them know without doubt that he was the undisputed boss. The best way to do this was to create a great new project for his hometown of Sukhumi, something so outrageously partisan that it was the best test of his power that he could devise.

Nesterov had come up with the idea. It was probably his greatest contribution to their friendship. It was typical of his limited intellect, so it suited Morozov's plan. They would build a big new building in Sukhumi, move all the computers and files from the Academy of Science to the building, and eventually construct a massive underground bunker as the final resting place for all the computer files, the greatest scientific treasure of the Soviet Union.

The uproar had been all that Morozov could have hoped for. One after another of his enemies opposed the scheme and ended up exiled to cities designed for dissidents and political prisoners. Gradually the Presidium took on the character that Morozov had anticipated. Finally no one opposed the move, and the building was completed at Sukhumi and the records were transferred.

The scientists had been secretly overjoyed, a fact Morozov had anticipated. They would be able to work far from the influence of Moscow, forgetting that nothing was far from the General Secretary and his precious monitors.

The KGB and the military had warned against the move because Sukhumi was not easy to defend. It was too close to the Turkish border and American air bases. It was on a seacoast where submarines could drop off spies. They presented every reason against the move, but when Morozov was adamant, they didn't press the issue. It would mean a bigger budget for them in the long run and that was, after all, their main objective.

"I was home last week, General Secretary," Nesterov said, using a more formal attitude while he was making a formal report. "The building is completed and the files have been moved."

"And the underground work?"

"About half finished," Nesterov said, pouring another vodka for himself.

"How long will the underground construction take?" the General Secretary asked.

"There are problems, General Secretary," Nesterov said, spilling some vodka on his suit and trying to wipe it off with a massive hand. "The rock is of great density. Many men have been lost in our rush to complete the work on schedule."

"Do you think I made a mistake, that we are too vulnerable?" Morozov asked.

"I was privileged to present the idea in the first place, Serge Federovich," Nesterov said with a broad grin, proud of himself. "I'm sure you took every factor into consideration," he added. He wasn't a total fool. He knew that his powerful friend had assigned their best people to provide total security for their hometown projects.

"I hope so, Misha. I hope so," the General Secretary said. Morozov knew better than anyone that it had been a power play and probably not a smart move. Now it had served its purpose. Perhaps it was time to build a new Academy of Science in Moscow and move all their valued computer work back to the safety of the capital city. Perhaps the battle had been won and it was time to be prudent. He was a hero to his fellow Georgians. They had their building and their underground project. They didn't have to know it was all temporary.

TWO

Cannes, July 18, 2:00 A.M.

The suite was small but elegant. Nick Carter had access to it whenever he was in Cannes. It was on the third floor of the club, looking out over the Mediterranean.

A full moon cast a glow that the water broke up into silver ripples, a wide path of glittering light that stretched as far as the eye could see.

Fresh from a shower and dressed only in a towel knotted at his waist, Carter turned from the window to look at the woman on the bed. She slept on her stomach, her body in a pose of abandon on the bed. Just looking at her brought back the sharp memory of their lovemaking. He felt himself becoming aroused again and shoved the thought of her restless body from his mind.

He had won ten thousand dollars. It was a small miracle. Someone had taught the twins to play. They were fast and they were good. His usual six hands a minute was cut to only four as they played as fast as he.

Mia had won more than Maria and had ended up in his bed. It was not by invitation but seemed to be preordained.

Maria simply vanished and Mia guided him to the elevator. She seemed to know where his suite was, and when they arrived he found that a magnum of champagne was on ice, waiting for them. Had he been a prize for the winner, the object of competitive women? He thought about it for all of five seconds and decided he didn't really care. The end justified the means.

The telephone rang. Carter rushed to the other room to answer before the sound disturbed the woman in his bed.

"How's the shoulder, Nick?" David Hawk's voice came at him loud and clear from the other side of the Atlantic. The usual gruffness was not there but the slightly slurred pronunciation was. Carter could imagine the battered cigar in one corner of his boss's mouth and could imagine the smell of the office or apartment where the older man was calling from.

"A bit stiff but getting better every day," Carter replied.

"Not too stiff for your favorite games, I trust."

Carter thought of Mia in the next room and the ten thousand held for him in the cashier's cage. "I'm getting by," he said.

"You always do. But I'm afraid the vacation's over."

"What's up?"

"No big rush this time. But I'd like you on the Concorde SST tomorrow. We've been asked . . . Oh, hell, I'll tell you about it when you get here. Be in my office tomorrow afternoon."

Carter turned to the door and walked to the other room, the towel falling from his hips.

Mia was sitting up in bed drinking champagne, her shoulders thrown back, her breasts jutting proudly, her whole demeanor bespeaking the proud heritage of a third-generation Greek shipping family. It had been obvious from the beginning that she and Maria had been to the finest schools, had unlimited funds at their disposal, and that they were accustomed to the best of everything.

"Business?" she said.

"Yes."

"You have to leave?" she asked, a note of regret in her voice.

"Not tonight."

She patted the bed beside her. He poured himself a glass of champagne and slid in next to her. She put down her glass and pushed her long dark hair behind her ears.

Carter put down his own glass and kissed her lightly.

Mia sighed. "I want you, but . . ." she started to say.

"But what?"

"But I'm . . . you know . . . still a bit worn out from before . . ."

He pulled her to him and held her close. "We don't have to make love all the time," he whispered into her ear. The truth was, he was tired too. He'd baked in the Mediterranean sun for the past few days and never seemed to be able to get enough sleep. On the last assignment he'd been trapped in the gulags deep within the Soviet and he'd been wounded on the way out. Sleep had been a luxury he wasn't allowed often enough.

As his eyes closed, he felt Mia's silky-smooth body move closer to him and hold him, every inch of her touching him, her skin like a furnace.

Soon, as sleep found him, he felt the hot breath of her mouth on his neck as she relaxed, caught up in the same lassitude as he.

He woke with a start. It was not unusual for him. Too many strange rooms and too many strange beds, usually alone in some remote corner of the globe.

As he moved his wrist to catch the light and read five minutes past six on his Rolex, the smell of expensive perfume wafted lightly to his nostrils. Then he felt the length of her against him, the hardening of her nipples against his back. Her hand snaked around his waist and took possession of him.

"I thought you were asleep," he said.

"Enough sleep," she whispered.

"You're not too tired?" he teased.

"I recover fast," she replied, moving down in the bed, her lips brushing his stomach.

He took her by the elbows and brought her up to him. They fitted together as if they had been created for each other. Her hands went around his neck. His circled her waist and settled on her magnificent breasts.

They found each other but didn't move at first. She raised her head and covered his mouth with hers. Her tongue sought his while magical inner muscles caressed him without her moving her body.

When she finally began to raise herself, the effect was like wafting fire over the most sensitive part of his body, scorching but not burning.

He felt himself begin to respond more quickly than he planned.

"Enjoy, enjoy!" she urged.

"It's too soon," he protested.

"Damn you! Let it come!" she demanded.

He felt the eruption start deep in his gut and rise like a thirty-foot wave to engulf them both. She rose with him, screaming out her joy, heightening his pleasure by tightening the muscles of her thighs and somehow making the caress cover every inch of him inside and out.

The outpouring of sensation was so pure and complete he couldn't breathe as he lunged under her. She matched his fury, pressing herself against him, draining him, screaming for more and when she got it, demanding more again and again.

It seemed like hours, but in minutes they lay side by

side, chests heaving, sweat glistening on their bodies. And, hands touching, they lay silently in the early morning light.

Nick Carter wasn't impressed by the SST and never had been. The Concorde had the advantage of not confining a seasoned traveler in a cabin any longer than necessary, but that cabin had been shrunk to claustrophobic proportions and gave him nothing to look at through the Coke-bottle windows.

Washington's Dulles Airport was a madhouse as usual. Carter walked off the aircraft with just one bag, took a cab to Dupont Circle, the headquarters of Amalgamated Press and Wire Services. He moved through the general offices that held legitimate press workers and took the elevator to the back. He palmed the flat identification plate outside two oak doors and walked in when the electronic lock clicked open.

"Nick!" the tall redhead said from behind a huge desk. Ginger Bateman was David Hawk's right hand and had been for years. She and Carter, once for a very brief time lovers, now had a deep and caring friendship. He knew that his long absences worried her, and because of her position she knew everything that happened to him. "You look great," she went on. "How's the arm?"

Carter struck a body-builder pose, flexing his arm. "All better," he told her, noting the fine lines at the corners of her mouth and eyes, signs of her concern and her involvement with men like him for too long. "How's the old man?"

"In a good mood. Go right in, he's expecting you."

As the door to Hawk's office opened, the foul smell of a cheap cigar escaped along with tendrils of smoke. The director of AXE was shorter than Carter by a head. He had a stocky build, clothed in a well-cut charcoal suit. His abundant white hair was unkempt as if he had been running his fingers through it.

"Come in, Nick," Hawk said, waving his top agent to the chair in front of his desk.

"Why did you call me back?" Carter asked, lighting a cigarette.

"A very unusual situation," Hawk said, getting up and pacing behind his desk. He finally stopped at a window, looked out at the traffic below, then turned to face Carter.

"The CIA has a defector who insists on talking to us," he said, blowing another cloud of smoke to the ceiling.

"That's a new one. How do they feel about it?"

"How do you think? They're furious. And I'm not too pleased myself. Let's face it, Nick, a Soviet dissident—a scientist—should not know that AXE exists."

Carter nodded but said nothing.

"They've had him for a month," Hawk continued. "They've got a lot from him, but they think they've only scratched the surface. That's why they're so pissed off that he wants to see us now."

"And they got him out. They're paying the freight for his relocation. Not an inexpensive operation," Carter observed. "Any clue as to what he wants?"

"Nope."

"How do you want to handle it?"

"It's all set up. They deliver him in an unmarked van to a parking lot at T Street and Nebraska Avenue," he said, throwing a key to Carter. "You take over at ten tomorrow morning and drive him to our place in Virginia."

Carter was all too familiar with the remote farm in Virginia where AXE conducted some of its training and put some of its people through a psychological assessment after a particularly tough assignment.

"Who's the Russian?" Carter asked.

"Viktor Mikhailovich Chestyakov," Hawk replied.

"The physicist?"

"The same."

Carter whistled. "A very big fish. How'd they get him?"

"Came over himself. With a whole squad of KGB guarding him, he slipped away from his hotel in Vienna and headed for our consulate."

"And the CIA got him out."

"While you were in Siberia. It was in all the papers. The General Secretary raised hell."

"Are you going to be there tomorrow?" Carter asked.

"Damned right. Just you and me and Howard."

Howard Schmidt was the man of all trades at AXE. Most of the time he sat in front of his computer console making sure that AXE was in the forefront of foreign agent identification. He was in charge of records. He had also developed a department of his own called "Innovations." Hawk hadn't liked what he'd called "Tomfoolery" at first, but when some of Schmidt's devices had saved agents' lives, Carter's included, Hawk was smart enough to give him his head. It wasn't a bad idea to have him on hand for the interrogation.

Carter slipped behind the wheel, started the Ford cargo van, and turned out onto Nebraska Avenue. When he headed west toward the Virginia countryside, a voice came at him from the other side of the grille that separated them.

"Carter?" the husky voice asked.

"I am Carter."

"You are the one who killed Margate the mole in Scotland?" the voice asked in Russian.

"How do you know about that?" Carter replied, also in Russian.

"The miniature atomic subs were my concept. They were intended for peaceful use."

"So much for the relationship between scientists and politicians," Carter said with disgust.

"Is it not the same in your country?" Chestyakov asked.

"I'm not the one to ask, Viktor Mikhailovich. All too often I have work to do because Soviet politicians guide the thinking of Soviet scientists," he said.

The man in back was silent for the rest of the trip.

The farmhouse sat back from the road on a ninety-acre spread. The approach road was lined with trees and shrubbery, the boughs of which intertwined to form an inpenetrable barrier. Within the greenery a twelve-foot-high chain link fence was topped with electrified barbed wire. Around the rest of the perimeter no attempt was made to hide the fence. Canine patrols and laser beams supplemented the fence to keep intruders out.

The house was still much as the farm family had left it. It was not large, but it was roomier than the average house. Most recruits and people in for refresher courses lived in bunkhouses discreetly situated deep within foliage-covered areas.

Hawk and Schmidt waited in the main room where four easy chairs had been pulled up in a circle around a table filled with soft drinks and liquor bottles.

"I work with these two men," Carter explained. "David Hawk is our director and Howard Schmidt runs our records department." He did not bother to introduce Chestyakov.

"Ah. I have read James Bond, Mr. Schmidt," Chestyakov said in English. "You are the one who builds the miniature cameras and the cars that shoot rockets."

Schmidt grinned and shook his head. Hawk looked annoyed. He had no sense of humor when the merits of his agency were discussed. But he was a realist. Nothing would be gained by antagonism. He poured the Soviet citizen a vodka and twisted a few drops of lemon into the glass.

"Mr. Hawk does his homework, Mr. Carter. He remembers more than any bartender I have met," Chestyakov said with a laugh as he accepted the glass. "But I can see he is most eager to get to business. I do not blame him," the Soviet scientist added. He was a big man, muscle rather than fat. He had a mane of dark brown hair and a full, almost unkempt beard. The eyes that stared out of wrinkled sockets were bright. The weight of his decision and the difficulties of the escape had not dulled them.

"I have made a decision, gentlemen. I will not work for you," he stated. "I will not help make weapons that will kill my own people."

THREE

The office of Nikolai Gladkov, the KGB security chief at Sukhumi, was in an old house taken over by preceding KGB officials from one of the more affluent members of the community. The original furniture stood like silent sentinels, bound to do his will. The original occupant's pictures graced the walls, expensive copies of old masters. The library had become his office. The rows of books, some proscribed by the Kremlin, still sat gathering dust on countless shelves.

Gladkov was a colonel, recently promoted for his work in Poland during some recent troubles. He was a tall man, well muscled, handsome in a rugged way. His rise within the Komitet had been rapid. He was a ruthless man, the kind that the General Secretary required for a sensitive installation.

"Tell me about the radar again," he asked his aide. "How did we allow it to be installed with a flaw?"

"The responsibility was given to the scientists," the tall young man said. He stood at attention in front of Gladkov's desk. He had never been invited to relax or sit in all the time he'd known his chief. "I'm not sure if the fault was

16

deliberate or an accident. Anyone could see the problem after only preliminary tests."

"Bring the man to me," Gladkov demanded. "We'll soon learn if it was an accident."

"It was Chestyakov, Colonel."

The man behind the desk smashed his fist against the polished surface. "That damned defector? Then it was no accident, you fool. Chestyakov sabotaged our radar. I want a new installation within days, do you hear? Within days!"

"Do you have any suggestions, Colonel?" the young aide asked, his knees giving him trouble.

"Where is the flaw?"

"To the northwest. A massive hill that rises well above the town."

"Then put the new installation on the hill. Do I have to think of everything around here?"

Viktor Chestyakov downed the vodka in one swallow and reached for the bottle. He didn't bother with the lemon juice. From here on it was the fiery liquid straight and often. "I warn you," he said. "I have had enough questions from your CIA to last a lifetime. This meeting is going to be short and to the point.

"You asked to see us," Hawk reminded.

"Ah. The hawk spreads his wings." The big Russian laughed. "I like that," he said in his heavily accented English.

"I came to you because of Carter," he said, moving closer to the head of AXE, his nose not ten inches away. "After the incident in Scotland when he destroyed all my shiny new toys, I made inquiries about him."

"We're aware of Carter's abilities," Hawk said without emotion. "You're the one straying from the point now."

"Not at all. Much is known about the great Killmaster in

Moscow. I decided that he was my man if ever I could escape."

"Your man for what?" Carter asked.

"All in good time," Chestyakov said slowly, draining his glass. He reached inside his pocket for a gnarled old pipe, tamped down the used tobacco, snapped a match across his thumbnail, and puffed contentedly. When he had the pipe going to his satisfaction, he smiled and leaned back, looking at each man in turn.

"The General Secretary has flexed his muscles politically and made the biggest blunder in recent Soviet history," he said, continuing to grin.

"And you're going to tell us what that is," Hawk said, his face still expressionless.

"Patience, Mr. Hawk. Patience. Until five weeks ago I was working at a new installation in a town in Georgia on the Black Sea coast. A town called Sukhumi. It's Morozov's hometown, the place where he started his rise to power," the big man said. "The General Secretary is not a fool, but he made a bad error of judgment."

"What is your assessment?" Carter asked. He still wasn't sure what the man was getting at, but he sensed it was something big.

"The Academy of Science in Moscow is overcrowded, or was. Morozov had a new Academy built in Sukhumi. All our best brains are now living there."

"And our CIA doesn't know about it?" Hawk asked incredulously.

"It is top secret, the information closely guarded."

"How do the scientists feel about it?" Schmidt asked.

"It's like a permanent vacation to them," Chestyakov said. "The Black Sea. Far from the pressures of Moscow."

"But the men and women of science don't see the whole picture," Hawk said.

"You are quick," Chestyakov said, nodding. "I see why

you are in charge. And you are right. Only a few of us really saw the danger. We agreed that one of us should make the break."

"To tell us of the weakness," Carter finished.

"To tell only Nick Carter and the man who controls him of the danger," Chestyakov said. "This opportunity cannot be lost by the bungling CIA. They are almost as bad as our cement-headed KGB."

"So tell us now," Hawk said, no longer able to control his impatience.

"They have brought in the toughest KGB colonel they have. Security is doubly tight. But not too tight for a man like Carter. Not if what I hear is correct."

"And what is that?" Carter asked.

"Every important scientific development in the past ten years is on magnetic tape and all at Sukhumi," the big Russian said, his eyes aglow with the telling. "And both the original tapes and backup are in the same building."

"I can't believe they would be that stupid," Hawk said, shaking his head.

"Believe it," Chestyakov said. "They are building an underground bunker for storage, but that won't be ready for months."

"You mentioned others," Carter said. "Who are they? If I go in, will they help?"

"Now, hold on, Nick," Hawk said. "No one said you were going in. We'll discuss that in private."

"You don't trust me?" Chestyakov accused.

"Mr. Chestyakov," Hawk said evenly, "the KGB has been setting traps to get at Carter for years. This could be the best one yet."

"You think I would come all this way to trap one agent?" the Russian asked. His face was flushed a deep red.

"Could be," Hawk said. "This could just be the icing for

you. The CIA have had you for more than a month. Why didn't you insist on seeing us first?"

"I did. Every day I insisted on seeing you. They refused. I understand your President intervened."

"Who are the others, Chestyakov?" Carter asked again. "We can do some checking before we move. Why don't you tell us all you can now?"

Chestyakov knocked the dregs out of his pipe into a big glass ashtray, filled the bowl with fresh tobacco, and flamed it. Hawk chewed the end off a fresh cigar and added to the clouds of smoke in the room. Carter lit one of his custom-blended cigarettes in self-defense. Schmidt waved the clouds of smoke away from his face and tried to concentrate.

"Nadya Karpova is a brilliant computer scientist. She will help," Chestyakov told them. "Filip Igor Pavlov is a physicist. We could not all get out. Mr. Carter will bring them out with him."

"How do you propose I get in?" Carter asked.

"If he goes at all," Hawk added quickly.

"I grow weary of your doubt, Mr. Hawk," Chestyakov said. He looked tired. His face was drawn. "I have just endangered the lives of two close friends. I am not going any further with this unless you make some kind of a commitment."

Hawk looked at him severely beneath bushy gray eyebrows. "If this is genuine, naturally we'll take a crack at it. I'll do some checking first, and I will not endanger your friends. But I will not send my best man into a trap."

"That is fair," Chestyakov said, puffing on his pipe. "I will answer Mr. Carter's question first."

"On how he might get in?" Schmidt asked.

"Exactly. They have a weakness in their security," the big man said confidently. "I set up the radar. I deliberately left a blind spot northwest of the town. It will be weeks before they can install a new scanning system."

"You're telling us that Nick can be dropped north of town without detection?" Hawk asked.

"Exactly. The land is rugged, uninhabited. He can set up a base ten miles out of town and never be discovered. All patrols are around the perimeter only."

"What about helicopter surveillance?" Schmidt asked. "How does he get back and forth? Ten miles is a long hike."

"Helicopters patrol once a day. You'd have to use a cave or camouflage," Chestyakov said. "As for the transport, that's your problem. It would be no problem for James Bond."

"This is not make-believe, Mr. Chestyakov," Hawk snapped. "This is real life and we bleed real blood here."

"The transport may not be a problem," Howard Schmidt mused. "I'd like to know a lot more about the town and the surrounding countryside."

Hawk ground out his cigar in the ashtray and stood. "I'll leave you to it. Be sure to get all you can out of him," he said, looking first at Carter, then at Schmidt. "I'm heading back to Washington. Call me at the office."

Hawk slept fitfully that night, cut himself shaving, and was not in the best of moods when he arrived at his office the next morning. He snapped at subordinates and plowed through backed-up reports, trying to finish some work before his midmorning appointment. He wanted to believe Chestyakov. If Carter went in and was successful, it could be the coup of a lifetime. It could mean setting the Soviets back scientifically for ten years at least. It could even mean the end of the current regime. . . .

Dupont Circle, at the junction of New Hampshire and Massachusetts avenues, was not far from the State Department at 23rd and C streets, but the drive took his man more than forty minutes in heavy traffic. Hawk knew that the Secretary of State was overseas, but Stewart Freeman, the deputy he was to see, was an old hand at State, outlasting several administrations, and he'd been in the intelligence community with Hawk before that.

"What do you think?" Hawk asked after he'd recited all that Chestyakov had told him.

"Fits with a few bits and pieces I already have," Freeman said, his brow furrowing in thought. "First, the CIA's monitoring of all calls into and out of all ministries in Moscow show a sharp decline at the Academy of Science. We've had people in there as cleaners and they tell us the activity has slowed to a crawl. We were looking for the answers."

He paused while a male secretary came in with a tray of coffee and sweet rolls. He poured, took a roll, and carried on. "Second, our satellite pictures show a new building at Sukhumi. We've been trying to get a line on it for a long time. It's about two years old. It's surrounded by what looks like groups of apartments, as if a lot of people have been transferred in. We lost two men in the last year trying to get close."

"What made you suspicious?" Hawk asked.

"Any oddity has to be checked out," the deputy said through a mouthful of Danish. "A new building, a sizable building in a place like Sukhumi, is an anomaly. And all the new accommodations. What's it all for?"

"My man says it's the hometown of the General Secretary," Hawk said. "Could it be strictly political? Something like a bone to throw his old friends?"

"Maybe. But they don't waste a building that size and they don't need one in Sukhumi," the deputy offered. "They're using it for something special."

"If we do go in, do you have anything you want us to find out?" Hawk asked.

"First, I definitely want you to find out if your defector's information is correct," Freeman said. "From what little we do know about what's going on down there, it would seem that what the defector brought you is authentic, but we have to be sure."

"What about the underground digs?" Hawk asked, finishing off his coffee and lighting one of his ever-present cigars.

The deputy was used to his old friend's habits. He switched on an air cleaner beside his desk. "It fits," he said. "The Soviets could be vulnerable as hell. They might plan to shift the computer records to underground vaults, but that takes time."

"I'm confused," Hawk admitted. "Chestyakov also speculates that the General Secretary could be moving the whole operation back to Moscow soon."

"He could be right. But they'd have to build a place to house them in Moscow first. As I said, all this takes time. They're not efficient builders. He could have a couple of years."

"You want to take the chance?" Hawk asked.

"No way. If this is the real thing, I want it all destroyed," Freeman said, a smile on his face. "Soon."

"Yes, Stuart, I agree."

"So he goes in now," Freeman said, sitting forward, his expression grim. "And there's something else I want."

"I don't think I'm going to like this," Hawk said, knowing his friend.

"It'll be a damned shame to destroy it all. It'll put the Soviets back at least ten years—but *we* might be able to use it."

"What do you mean?" Hawk asked, afraid he already knew.

"We know they've been working on their own version of 'star wars.' We also know they could be way ahead of us—making a big show at the arms meetings and moving ahead of us in secret."

"Sounds like them," Hawk agreed.

"I want your man to select a few of their most recent developments and send them back to us by modem."

Hawk was silent for a few moments, then looked straight at Freeman. He'd seen Carter do more miraculous things in the past, but this assignment would truly be placing his number one operative smack in the lion's—or rather the bear's—mouth. "Where does he send the data?" he asked at last.

"A carrier in the Aegean. An agent in Istanbul. Who knows? We'll have to set it up," the deputy said.

"One last thing," Hawk said. "We want copies of all your satellite shots. No later than tomorrow."

Carter and Schmidt had spent another couple of hours with Chestyakov drawing a street map of the town and a fairly accurate topographical of the ground within fifteen miles. Fortunately the immediate area was relatively deserted. A good road joined in to towns to the north and south. The sea was at its doorstep. But the surrounding rocky terrain, spotted here and there with high ridges of rock, was not inhabited.

The CIA had come for Chestyakov and interrupted the discussion.

"A few more minutes, please," Chestyakov begged. "I must see Mr. Carter alone."

Carter nodded to the others and they trooped out of the house.

"I'll wait for you out front," Schmidt said.

When they were alone, Chestyakov didn't waste any time. "I am afraid for my friends," he said. "I am not lying to you, Carter, I swear. If you go in and destroy the tapes, much of my work will be destroyed, but at least we will have preserved world peace. That is why I came out. That and to find a way to get my friends out."

"I can't make promises—" Carter started.

The big man raised his hand to interrupt. "I know. Your boss will decide. But if you go, I want your promise that you will bring out my friends."

"If I go, I will do my best for them," Carter said.

Chestyakov slumped in an overstuffed chair. The life seemed to go out of him as if he'd spent all his energy, had been staving off exhaustion until that moment. "Tell them to come in," he said. "Tell the jackals to come in again."

The next day, in Howard Schmidt's domain in the basement of Amalgamated Press and Wire Services, at about the time that Hawk took off for State, Schmidt was sounding off while Carter still thought about his commitment to Chestyakov.

"You're not listening," Schmidt complained. He had pictures of Nikolai Gladkov and Nadya Karpova on the desk in front of him. He'd found a file on each of them and had been bringing Carter up to date. "I don't have a thing on Pavlov. We may have to talk to Chestyakov again."

"Forget Chestyakov. I doubt if they'll let us see him again," Carter said. "What about Sukhumi? I need at least one diversion. Any ideas?"

"What have you got in mind?"

"When I'm trying to destroy the tapes, and I'm not sure how, I'll need the building and surrounding area cleared for at least two hours."

Schmidt sat for a minute, his chin supported by one hand. Carter had seen this attitude before. It usually ended with some brilliant deduction or plan.

"Got it!" Schmidt said. He left for a minute or two and came back with a strange-looking box.

"What the hell is that?" Carter asked.

"When assembled it will look exactly like an atomic bomb. Every rivet shows. All the decals look authentic." He handed Carter a can of spray paint. "After you build it, use this aluminum spray. They'll never know the difference."

"You're crazy. For one thing, the model will be too light."

"So you fill it with sand or whatever's handy."

"It doesn't have a decent timing mechanism."

Schmidt left again for a couple of minutes. He came back with an electronic timing device that was the real thing. "You strap this on, use the glue to make it look neat. You just key in the time you want and push this button," he said, pointing.

Strangely enough, Carter had dealt with Howard Schmidt enough to realize that it would work. "What do you figure we should use for transport?" he asked, the matter of the diversion settled.

"Come on. My other lab. The one I keep closed," Schmidt said, leading the way.

At the far corner of Schmidt's bailiwick he kept a lab behind locked doors. He changed the lock combinations every couple of days. He used the latest codes, whisked Carter in, and closed the door quickly. The room's floor, ceiling, and bare walls were of unpainted cement. Fluorescent lights were fitted between overhead piping. It looked very ordinary except for the long wooden tables covered with piping, motors, gasoline cans, and what looked like an open parachute.

"What is it?" Carter asked.

"I'm not sure," Schmidt began, "but I do know some things it will do. But . . ."

Carter stood back as the genius of AXE started to fit

some pipes together. When he had a kind of framework assembled, he fitted an enlarged bicycle seat in place, used two large and two small wheels to make it look something like a dune buggy, then screwed on a gas tank, a four-horse motor and chain drive. When he'd finished placing the steering gear, he stood back and said, "Your own personal ATV. I've tried this much. It holds together over some pretty rough terrain."

"What do you mean, 'this much'?" Carter asked cautiously.

Schmidt grinned. He moved the gas tank to the framework over the driver's head, then assembled the motor beside it. He pulled a lightweight aluminum propeller from beneath a canvas tarpaulin and screwed it in place. The thing that looked like a parachute was actually a hang glider sail. Schmidt fastened it on a post projecting from the frame and stood back.

"Son of a bitch!" Carter breathed. "Does it work?"

"That, I haven't been able to try," Howard admitted. He looked at the assembled ultralight aircraft proudly. "I don't see why not. The theory is right."

"Jesus!" was all Carter could say.

"The horizontal tubing on the sides has brackets to take portable surface-to-air missiles or antitank rockets," Howard explained. "You can use the SAMs on the ATV if you can stop and elevate them enough. On the ultralight, I don't know. Could be too unstable."

"I don't think I'll try it."

"Well, I'll put them in the package anyway. I've made a full set of notes, a kind of manual on what the whole pile of stuff will do. This all fits into a smaller package than you'd think. Easy enough for a chopper to take in. No sweat."

Carter just stood, looking at his friend in the cold, bare

room. "No sweat," he muttered almost to himself. "No sweat. I just hope it's no sweat when I've got to use it."

"Just give me a call if you have any trouble," Schmidt said, grinning, slapping his friend on the shoulder. "I'm listed under AAA."

FOUR

Somewhere in the Aegean, July 21.

Captain Martin Jameson of the USS *Ticonderoga* sat in the luxurious commanding officer's suite of one of the Navy's newest and most modern aircraft carriers. He was going over the latest orders received from COMATFLT with his first officer. While he came under the command of the admiral commanding the Atlantic fleet, his ship was far from the Atlantic Ocean.

"It really pisses me how some intelligence people we don't know can order us to put a spook in place," Gerry Orwell said, taking off his cap and placing it on a chair beside him.

The steward hung the cap on a peg near the door and carried a tray of ice and frosted glasses to the table beside them. The suite was huge by Navy standards. In the modern Navy, only the captains of battle carriers and the flag officers of a task force rated such accommodation.

"Don't let it get to you, Gerry," the captain said. "They build carriers to control the seas, but sometimes we're the best tool they have to put a man in place."

"One man. That's what gets me. One damned man. What the hell could be so important?"

"Don't kid yourself. One man can make one hell of a difference," Jameson said, taking one of the tall glasses and drinking half the cool liquid in one swallow. "How'd you like to be dropped behind enemy lines and operate alone for weeks?"

"No way," Orwell said, following the captain's lead with the drinks. "You have to be some kind of nut to take that on."

"Then we follow orders and do all we can for the guy," Jameson said, lighting a long, slim cheroot. "One of our Tomcats is returning from the repair depot on Cyprus. They're putting the guy in the second seat. Should be here tonight."

"What about his gear?" Orwell asked.

"Coming in on a Seahawk. One hell of a pile of gear for a spook. We'll have to use one of our Seahawks equipped with long-range tanks to take him in. The delivery's on the western shore of the Black Sea."

"We don't need long-range tanks for that."

Jameson held out the orders for Orwell to read. "Catch the last few sentences," he said. "Got to fly in from the east at a specific bearing to take advantage of a blind spot in their radar."

"Someone's been doing his homework," Orwell suggested.

"Or someone set it up that way," the captain said, pulling himself from the comfortable chair and heading for a chart table on the far bulkhead. "Look at this. Our guy's got to follow the Turkish shore of the Black Sea to Batumi, the first Georgian town in the USSR across the border. He's got to fly low for a hundred and fifty miles to the Caucasus around Mestia."

"He'll have to stay on the east side of the ridge heading

north to Teberda, then hop back over the mountains and come in low to Sukhumi," Orwell finished for his captain. "A hell of a flight."

"Too far for the long-range tanks."

"We can pick him up on the way back. Let's see. Around a Turkish town called Hopa. We can refuel him en route."

The captain figured the distance and load. "Can be done if he doesn't face headwinds most of the time. Maybe fifteen minutes to spare before we can pick him up."

"Shit!" Orwell whispered. "We ask for volunteers?"

"You won't have any problems. Our pilots are all bored as hell. They haven't had anything exciting since our NATO exercise last month." He thought about it for a moment. "Maybe we should play it safe—ask Charlie Dahl for their best."

Commander Dahl was the Seahawk squadron commander, a friend of Orwell's. The first officer picked his cap from the peg. "I think I'll go talk to him now," he said.

When Orwell had gone, Jameson sat alone in his luxurious quarters. Men like Orwell had never seen the types who worked alone behind enemy lines. The spooks were a breed apart. He wondered about the man coming in on one of his Tomcats. Would he be like the others? The ones he'd seen on other missions kept to themselves, were introspective and uncommunicative.

All except one. He'd taken one named Carter into the Gulf of Finland and dropped him not far from Leningrad a couple of years ago. That one had been different—human, conversational, bright, and lively to the last minute they were together. He had never seen the man again, but somehow he knew that Carter was a survivor.

"What about uniforms?" Schmidt asked in the last minutes that Carter spent at Dupont Circle. "I've got just about any Soviet type you could want."

"A major from the Inspector General's Office usually opens doors," Carter said. "Maybe a captain of the Kremlin Guards. I could be an aide to the General Secretary on special assignment."

"Anything else? What about civilian clothes?"

"A pea jacket, old jeans, and black knitted hat. It's basically a seaport. I'll probably hang around the docks. You'd better make sure the seaman's clothes stink."

"Have you seen Hawk since the farm?" Schmidt asked.

"No. I've got all the input I'm going to get. It's all up here," Carter said, tapping his head. "How are you getting me to the drop site?"

"Air Force jet to Cyprus. Navy Tomcat to the USS *Ticonderoga*. Helicopter the rest of the way. I don't know what kind they're using."

"Doesn't matter."

Schmidt turned from what he was doing and faced his longtime friend. "Take care of yourself, Nick," he said. "This one's gonna be tricky."

Carter had been busy for the last two hours. He hadn't taken time for a smoke. Until his base was established and he'd done a recon of his perimeter, he wasn't about to have cigarette smoke giving him away.

Howard Schmidt hadn't missed a trick. He had provided enough uniforms, supplies, gimmicks, and armaments to satisfy a small army. Carter chuckled to himself when he thought about the cursing from the Seahawk crew when it came time to load and unload.

He thought about the supersonic flight to Cyprus. He never thought he would be bored with such a flight. He'd slept most of the way, hanging in his harness like a puppet between acts.

The captain of the carrier had seemed familiar. He was sure they had met before. This time Carter's total recall

failed him. Too many men with stripes on their sleeves
paraded before his eyes over the years. Unless they had
been an intricate part of an operation, all their faces
blended together.

Charlie Dahl he would remember. The sad-eyed commander of a squadron of Seahawks had been through the
mill. During the flight they hadn't exchanged war stories.
Between professionals, men who had been there and back,
the need to speak the words was not part of their makeup.

The big chopper had set him down about ten miles from
his objective. Between him and Sukhumi an imposing hill
of rock towered to more than fifteen hundred feet. Dahl's
keen eyes had found a shelf of rock leading to a cave. It
was big enough for him to set the chopper down. A path
from the cave to the valley floor was relatively smooth,
smooth enough for an ATV.

The two hours since the huge machine had lifted off and
disappeared into the night sky had been productive. Carter
had set up a pup tent inside the cave. A huge camouflaged
tarpaulin covered the entrance. Inside, the ATV had been
assembled, complete with the top framework and the SAM
missiles. He figured he'd never fire them against aircraft,
but they'd scare the hell out of anyone who came at him
from the front, whether he hit them or not.

It was time for a look-see. Carter checked his familiar
weapons. The 9mm Luger he called Wilhelmina was snug
in her holster under his left armpit. Hugo, his razor-sharp
stiletto, was in the chamois sheath strapped to his right
forearm. A special muscle twitch would cause a spring to
shoot its hilt into his palm in the blink of an eye. Last,
taped high on his inner thigh like a third testicle, nestled a
small, egg-shaped gas bomb he called Pierre. Sometimes
the tiny bomb was filled with debilitating gas; sometimes
the gas was lethal. This one contained a deadly gas that
would kill in a few seconds breathed in a confined space.

Carter always felt more comfortable when his old friends were in place. He had given them names when he was much younger and much more sentimental. The names had stuck and were still with him. He dressed in the soiled clothes of a seaman, slung a submachine gun over his shoulder, and stepped out of the cave to made a preliminary recon of the area.

The night was clear. The mountain air was crisp and slightly cool. Even in summer on the Back Sea shore, Carter was glad of the pea jacket. He knew that he would get used to the smell of its previous owner in time. Right now, with a breeze blowing in his face, the smell was minimal.

Carter skirted the oversize hill from his cave to the side facing the sea. He crawled from one boulder or shelf of rock to another. It had to be midnight when he stood on the west side of the hill looking out at the dark mass that was the sea in the distance.

Between him and the water, a dull glow told him that the town still showed some light. With the security he had been warned to watch for, light would be important. You don't provide first-class security in the dark.

Carter had as much night vision as the moon would allow. He scanned the horizon for other lights and found none. The terrain wouldn't support a farm or even a herd of sheep. He'd seen the odd mountain goat, but they were wild. He would not run into civilian interference between here and Sukhumi and that was one big plus.

The whole scene looked peaceful. It was too good to be true. They hadn't been detected on the way in or he'd have seen HI-24 choppers by now. They were the gunboats favored by the Soviets for surveillance.

Carter slipped the AK-80 Soviet automatic rifle from his shoulder and sat on a shelf of rock, his feet dangling in space. Howard Schmidt had supplied the new weapon along with everything else. He said an Afghan rebel had taken it from a Soviet recruit. Apparently it was a new model. It fired 5.45mm rounds from the usual orange-colored plastic-coated clips. This one was equipped with a night scope unfamiliar to him. He raised it to his shoulder and scanned the horizon.

Carter saw nothing out of the ordinary until he brought the scope to a part of the scene only a couple of miles away. At the foot of the hill he saw a pile of supplies and was able to follow a faint trail in the scrub brush back as far as Sukhumi. He scanned the material closely. It looked like an assembly kit for a huge radar dish. Someone had delivered it and had not yet installed it. He remembered Chestyakov's words: "It will be weeks before they can install a new scanning system." The man from AXE would have to keep clear of the installation and finish his project as soon as possible.

Carter moved back to the cave. He sat having his first smoke in hours, knowing he was safe from detection for now. He had slept too much in transit to be tired now. The adrenaline was flowing. He decided to head into town to see what he was up against.

The ATV was an awkward assembly of pipes and wheels, but it worked like a charm. Carter felt like an astronaut making it across uncharted moonscape except that the moon was lighting his way. He covered seven of the ten miles in an hour. He would have done much better, but detours made the journey more like twenty miles.

He found a fissure of rock big enough to hide the vehicle, unrolled a sheet of camouflage material, and hid the ATV completely. He left the AK-80 behind.

The walk to the edge of town was over hard ground, boulder-strewn, overgrown here and there with stunted brush. He came out of his cover to find himself in a new housing subdivision. The skeletons of new buildings looked like ghostly shapes against the sky. He had to hide in one to let a troop carrier pass by, its searchlights criss-crossing the wooden framework close to him.

The man from AXE was in his element. He was dressed in dark clothes. A bank of clouds had drifted in from the mountains covering the moon's light. The map of the town as drawn for him by Chestyakov was etched in his brain.

He moved from the new structures to the old town at Weilun Ulitsa, a street described to him as one with large old houses that the KGB and the military had taken over as their headquarters. Carter hid behind shrubbery that had been planted by former tenants and grown to maturity many years ago. He saw KGB headquarters and the house they used as a jail. He moved westward toward the sea and passed through Krasnaia Ploshad, the town's Red Square, and the original old municipal buildings.

Nester Bul'var on the west side of Red Square was a wide boulevard that led to the sea and rows of old houses along the docks. The whole area smelled of dead fish and rotting seaweed. A light shone in a window at street level. It had to be a seaman's bar. Even in Sukhumi, a town with incredible security, the seamen would have their way. Their favorite bars would be open twenty-four hours a day. Even Gorbachev's edicts on liquor consumption would not be enforced here.

Carter slid his well-worn jeans onto a barstool. One other sailor sat at the bar. One booth was occupied by three men who were totally overcome with drink. The place was small, large enough to serve thirty men, no more.

"What'll you have?" the huge man behind the bar asked. He was a bruiser with a nose that was almost flat to his face, his nostrils mere slits with hair protruding. He spoke with a Georgian accent.

"Vodka," Carter said. He used a Ukrainian accent. Most

of the seamen who plied the coastal waters were from
Odessa.

The barman poured a small glass.

"No damned good," Carter complained. "A bottle. A
whole damned bottle."

The bottle was thumped on the bar beside his money.
The bartender stood in front of him. "I don't know you,"
he said, his voice booming out like a cannon. "Where'd
you come from?"

"None of your damned business," Carter said, knowing
it was the response the bartender would usually get.

The other man at the bar sidled closer, taking the worn
stool next to Carter. The American filled his own glass and
noted the man smelled even worse than he. The bartender
smelled worse than either of them. Carter doubted if the
man ever bathed.

"Got a drink for a mate?" the sailor asked.

Carter poured the man's glass full, downed his own, and
filled it again. The bottle was half empty already.

"Bartenders are too fuckin' nosy," the man mumbled.
"What ship are you from?"

Carter told him he'd been on an ocean-going fishing
boat, but had slugged a mate and was put ashore. He was
looking for a berth.

"Aren't we all?" the sailor said.

"You want a bunk?" the bartender asked.

Carter expected the question. It was what he had come
to hear. Barmen the world over made money touting everything from women to flophouses. "Need some sleep," the
Killmaster said. "You got a room?"

"Not me."

"What do you plan to do ashore, comrade?" the drunken
sailor asked, interrupting.

"Get a room, alone. Find a woman. Find another woman."

The laughter of the man beside him filled the room. The others looked up and grinned.

"Ivan's place, up the hill to the right as you leave, maybe two hundred meters," the bartender told him. "Give you a room for three rubles a night. The women you'll have to find yourself," he said, picking up Carter's money and retreating to the end of the bar.

"You won't have any trouble, comrade. One who looks like you," the man beside him wheezed, holding out his glass for a refill.

Ivan had three rooms available. Carter chose one overlooking the docks. He examined the four-story building carefully, choosing windows for observation and routes for escape.

It was past six by the time he was settled in. He stayed in the area, ate in nearby cafés, and slept during the day. The town north of the port was active. Workmen returned to the wooden framework of the new housing. The sound of saws and drills filled the air.

When he finally woke, ready to make his first sortie, night had again descended over the port. The smell of fresh-cut wood was replaced by sea smells. The bars were all filled, the shouting and laughter of seamen and dockworkers was loud in the evening breeze.

Carter walked at leisure through the town, his pea jacket turned up against a stiff sea breeze. He walked three blocks inland and ambled past the new science building. It was fully a hundred yards long by fifty yards wide. The structure rose, a huge rectangular monolith, for six stories. Carter figured it could hold one hell of a lot of scientific equipment.

The apartment buildings were alive with people. These were not seamen or townspeople. They were intellectuals, out of their element in the small town but without realizing it. They seemed to be in a world of their own, deep within the walls they had created out of knowledge and the language of their calling.

At each building's entrance, a matronly woman sat at a plain desk, her eyes taking in everything around her. Carter knew that each building would have three or four such women on duty. It was part of the normal surveillance of one Soviet citizen by another, part of the huge mechanism that was the *Komitet Gosudarstvennoy Bezopasnosti*, the KGB.

Carter was the one out of place here. He knew that men from the rusty ships at anchor had no place among the newcomers. But alone, he had to get what intelligence he could, any way he could. If he didn't get it this way, he'd have to find other lodging, assume another identity, and blend in with the transplanted Muscovites.

"Your papers, comrade." A short man in a black overcoat had addressed him. Carter had not seen him approach. Another, a man in the uniform of an army corporal, stood by, a Kalashnikov slung over his shoulder.

Carter handed over his stained seaman's papers. His Luger felt like a dead weight under his armpit. The stiletto seemed like a foreign object against his forearm. If they went for a body search, he was in trouble.

"What are you doing here at night, comrade?" the KGB man asked.

"Fresh air," Carter said, using the slurred tongue of a sailor with too many beers in his gut. "Needed to get out. Too much booze. Feel dizzy."

"Come with us, comrade," the man in the black coat ordered. "We'll see if you are telling the truth."

A small Zhugili was parked down the street. Carter offered no resistance when they shoved him in the back of the car. The corporal got in with him, keeping the automatic rifle pointed at his chest.

They drove away from the new buildings toward the excavation and some older buildings that once belonged to the elite of the town. Carter guessed they were heading for the local KGB headquarters.

This was no time for that kind of luck. There was no way he could be locked up now. When they reached a dark street away from the busy heart of town, he knocked the corporal's weapon to one side and brought Hugo out and up in one fluid motion.

The long blade punctured the corporal's heart, and the big man collapsed against Carter without a sound. The Killmaster pushed the body to one side, cleaned off Hugo on the man's rough khaki uniform, and traded him for Wilhelmina. He stuck the Luger's barrel into the KGB man's neck and whispered in his ear, "Pull into the nearest alley or I'll blow your head off."

The driver complied. Carter couldn't see his face or read what was in his eyes, and he wasn't sure if the man would try something. He kept the gun pressed to his neck until they had come to a stop in the darkness of an alley.

"Out!" he ordered.

The KGB man slid from the front seat and went for his heavy Makarov pistol, the standard KGB handgun.

Carter had no choice. He had to shoot. With the small man partway out of the car, the 9mm slug caught him in the temple and blew his brains against the alley wall.

The car was still relatively clean. He dumped the KGB man in the back seat next to the corporal, and drove carefully to the site of the tunnel excavation. Carter could not see anyone following the car, and assumed no one had heard the shot.

Carter searched the trunk and found an empty canvas sack. He stripped both men and folded their clothes into the bag. He had just thrown their bodies into an empty dump truck and was heading for the car when someone else joined the action.

"Halt!" a deep bass voice commanded.

A guard, dressed in the uniform of an army private, came at him, his automatic rifle held at the ready.

"What are you doing here? What did you toss in the truck?" he demanded.

Carter went for his Luger, but the big man swung his rifle butt and knocked the Killmaster down. He was about to raise the alarm when Carter's boot caught him in the groin. The big man doubled over, the rifle falling in the dirt at his feet. His knees started to buckle and his hands went to his groin.

Still groggy from the rifle butt's crushing blow, Carter caught the private by his collar and started to hoist him into the truck with the others. A massive fist caught him in the gut, driving the wind from him for a moment.

The guard was on his knees. His mouth was open as if to scream out a warning. Only mewling sounds emerged as the man's crushed testicles announced their pain, the agony coursing through his body.

Carter struggled to his feet. Hugo was in his hand as if by magic. He couldn't take any more chances with this one. He silenced the man's whimpering with one thrust of the blade between unguarded ribs. The he tossed the body into the truck and stood erect, listening.

He heard nothing. The man he had killed had been the only one on duty. The spot was deserted at night, apparently of no strategic value. He slid behind the wheel of the car and drove it to a dark part of town, wiped it clean of his fingerprints, and walked casually back to Ivan's, his rucksack still over his back.

FIVE

"Tell me the whole story again," he told his aide. "I don't believe it could happen here."

"Believe it," the captain said. "One of our men, an old hand, was shot and dumped in a truck. A corporal who accompanied him on night duty was knifed, his body dumped in the same truck." He paused to light a cigarette, his hand shaking in the process. "A guard at the tunnel excavation was knifed by a very sharp and long weapon. His body was also dumped in the same truck. If the operator hadn't planned to inspect his truck the next morning, he wouldn't have found them. They would have been part of the landfill site."

Gladkov sat glowering out a dusty window, stroking his unshaven chin.

"Someone is out there. Someone is about to challenge us," he said pensively. "The General Secretary warned us and demanded we double the guard. Was this done?"

"No, Comrade Colonel. The orders were just being cut," the captain said, his knees shaky.

"Do it now! Within the hour!" he screamed at his aide. "And have them bring around my car. I want to see for myself what this intruder has accomplished."

The captain left in a hurry, his heels clicking on the hard floors, the sound slowly disappearing. Gladkov opened a drawer and took out a bottle of vodka. He poured a few ounces in a glass and gulped the contents in one swallow.

So it has begun, he thought. *Someone, some enemy, has finally caught on to this political madness and the race to destroy it has begun.*

He poured another three fingers and sat, the fiery liquid burning as it slid down his throat. Okay. He had dealt with this kind of thing before. He was usually able to put himself in an adversary's mind and anticipate what he would do next.

What would he do next? he asked himself. Or was it a she? Was it a well-organized gang? He would know soon and he would deal with them. He would deal with them his way, not the scientific way. He was tired of all the scientific mumbo jumbo he heard every day now. No. This would be simple. He would find the enemy and force him, or them, to talk.

He would do it the hard way.

The room at Ivan's was rank. Previous tenants had cooked in the room. The smell of boiled cabbage permeated the walls and the soiled coverings of overstuffed chairs. The painted walls were peeling. With every vibration, minuscule flakes of green paint dropped, adding to the film of dirt already on the floors.

Carter examined the uniform he had stolen. The knife hole was not a problem. The blood on the Khaki tunic could be removed. The shirt was soaked in blood but it would do. He cut the cuffs free and the collar, including the yoke at the top of the shirt. The cuffs he taped to his wrists. The upper portion stayed on his shoulders when he put on the tunic. The cuffs looked normal.

The contents of the pockets were interesting. The soldier had a wallet containing pictures of him and his family. He'd had only a few rubles. The man was bearded, but Carter could fix that. The only item he could not use was some kind of identity card that was so covered with blood he couldn't even read it.

The tunic dried in a few hours. Late in the day with less than an hour of light, Carter dressed, checked his appearance against the picture, and sneaked out the back way, the Kalashnikov slung over his shoulder. He had twenty rounds left in the banana clip that was built for thirty, and two full clips in his webbing.

The bearded American in the Russian corporal's uniform started his prowl for information. Behind a guard post on Morozov Naberezhnaya, the coastal embankment named after the General Secretary, Carter found an old motorcycle unattended. It looked like a Harley Davidson, probably copied from the original design. It seemed to be roadworthy. He checked the gas tank. It was half full, good for at least a couple of hours of steady riding.

Carter wheeled the machine a half block from the post, started it, and cruised east on the embankment toward the new part of town. He found that the old town was probably a half-mile square, bordered by Katowice Prospekt on the east, Sukhumi Prospekt on the west, a row of old houses on Novoza Prospekt to the north, and the embankment on the south. Ivan's rooming house was at the southwest corner of the old town, on the embankment, a few doors from Sukhumi Prospekt.

The new science center was in the northwest quadrant of the old town. It was surrounded by new apartment buildings, all six stories high. They contained forty or fifty apartments each, enough to house five hundred scientists or the same number of families.

The southeast quadrant was the most disreputable, filled

with houses like Ivan's for transient seamen or people with only two or three rubles between them and a night out in the cold.

The most imposing structures were the old mansions along Novoza Prospekt to the north. Each had a new sign out front announcing the headquarters for the KGB, or the army, or the navy. One, at the corner of Novoza Prospekt and Katowice Prospekt, had been converted to a jail. A fitting symbol of the prosperity of the town.

Behind these old mansions, all commandeered for official use, the hills rose into a low mountain range. Building here was sparse. The tunnel for the repository was at the west end of this hilly area.

To the east and west of the old town, new houses were being built in profusion for the families dispossessed by the influx of officialdom, or for those who had come in as new workers. The face of the town had obviously undergone a drastic change.

Carter drove the old bike sedately up and down every thoroughfare of the old town, stopping to look over the jail, the KGB headquarters, the new science building, and the hundreds of new apartments, some occupied and others still vacant. These were of special concern. The tour was only a beginning, the initial recon. He still had to learn where the most important files were stored, identify the ones he wanted to send back to Washington, and the ones he was ordered to destroy.

He knew his time was limited. When he passed the dump trucks at the north end of town, they had already found the bodies. The KGB was out in force. His knew his life wouldn't be worth a plugged nickel if he was discovered now.

Carter stopped and leaned the machine against a post while he lit a cigarette, a Russian weed that was bitter and hot to the throat.

"Corporal," a voice behind him said. "What are you doing with that machine at this time of the day?" An officer walked around in front of him, his eyes cold and demanding.

"I'm a dispatcher. I just delivered a message to the commandant." Carter said the first thing that came into his head.

"Wrong answer," the officer said, a wicked grin spreading over his face. He was tall and muscular, and wore a KGB Special Guards uniform. "Messages are sent by modem or teletype, Corporal. All officers carry beepers.

"Guard! Arrest this man!" he shouted to unseen help.

Carter silenced the officer with a quick thrust to the heart. He withdrew Hugo and turned to the bike, but it was demolished by a stream of 7.62mm slugs from a submachine gun. The fuel tank blew, throwing Carter to the road. He scrambled up, unslung his Kalashnikov, and got off a three-round burst in the general direction of the unseen enemy.

No one fired again, but Carter realized he was now extremely vulnerable in the street. He ran toward a group of trees to the south side of the street, slid behind one, and watched the area around the burning bike.

Carter heard the snapping of a twig behind him. He started to turn, and something crashed into the back of his head. The pain lasted only a second or two as everything changed from spots of light to black.

The light that shone in his eyes was so bright that it hurt. He was naked to the waist, strapped to a chair.

"So the killer of my men joins us at last," a voice said coldly.

Carter turned toward the voice. His eyes focused. He saw a military man, an officer wearing the bars of a colonel. He was in full uniform, including his hat and an officer's baton. This was a man of order and precision, a man in his fifties, a career soldier or a dedicated KGB man. Either way, Carter knew he spelled trouble with a capital *T*.

"We will not discuss innocence or guilt here," the sharp-featured colonel continued. "You were dressed in the uniform of the corporal you killed. We have witnesses who saw you kill Captain Berghov.

"A nice touch, the collar and the sleeves. I wouldn't have thought of that," the colonel continued, obviously liking the sound of his own voice. "It proves you are a man of resources, a man accustomed to subterfuge. But you made mistakes," he went on, his voice a monotone. "You had no warrant. I insist every man carry a special warrant card issued by me alone."

So that was the blood-covered card the corporal was carrying, Carter thought.

"Bring in the other one!" the colonel shouted without pause.

Two military men pulled a reluctant Ivan into the room. His face was covered in blood. He had fewer teeth than when Carter had seen him last. He fell to the floor near Carter's feet.

"You told this man you came from a ship. He told us the name of the ship. We've talked to some of the men who sailed on that ship," the colonel continued his recital. "They never heard of you. You are a spy and we know what you're here for," he said, his mouth close to Carter's ear.

Carter said nothing. Ivan's information wouldn't help or hurt Carter's cause. So far, they had done nothing to him. His head hurt from the rifle butt that had downed him earlier, but the pain was not unbearable.

The colonel nodded and one of the soldiers smashed Ivan's head with his rifle. It was a crushing blow. The sound was startlingly loud. Blood gushed from the man's nose and mouth.

"He was just a landlord," Carter protested.

"It doesn't matter to me. One life is nothing." The colonel raised his voice for the first time. He seemed to be working himself into a frenzy. Carter guessed that playing games with his prisoners was the only amusement he could find here.

The colonel nodded to the corporal, who pounded the landlord's head with the rifle until the blows were landing on pulp.

"Take him away and mop up this mess," the colonel said. He stood, smoking, the baton under one arm, shifting his feet, while men dragged the body out and others mopped the floor.

Carter knew that the ploy was psychological. He was more a master of this situation than his enemy. It didn't matter that he was the captive and the enemy was in control. He understood his position. If they didn't need to know all he could tell, he would be eliminated by now. They had him dead to rights on the killings.

"A man appears from nowhere and kills four of our people before he is caught. He carries very special weapons into the country," the colonel said, producing the Luger and the stiletto and shoving them into Carter's face.

"Such a man can have only one purpose," the colonel said. "You are a spy, a saboteur. You were sent here by the United States to destroy our installations."

"To hell with you!" Carter spat. "To hell with you and your bungling KGB," he went on, baiting the man into a fury. He'd had enough of the colonel's cold rationality. He'd be better off if the KGB officer was just mad and out for revenge.

"I warn you!" the colonel screamed. "I am Nikolai Ivanovitch Gladkov, attached to the Fifth Directorate—"

"Central Control for Regional Units," Carter finished for him. "You must have been a bad boy to be sent to this hole."

"This hole? This is one of the most import—" Gladkov started to say and choked off the rest of it.

He swung on Carter. The baton caught the Killmaster on the side of his face, raising an ugly welt. The colonel stood back, his eyes blazing, as he nodded to one of the men who stood beside the prisoner.

Carter steeled himself for a beating. He knew the routine all too well. This one was from the old school and he thanked the gods of war that it was so. A beating he could take. He had proved a hundred times that no one could make him talk under physical torture. It was the mind-bending drugs that he feared. They could cause permanent damage, the shortening of a career or a life.

The guard struck him with a fist covered with a heavy leather glove. His head snapped back and he felt a tooth loosen at the side of his mouth. He sat erect, looking straight ahead, feeling the loose tooth with his tongue.

The colonel nodded again. The fist crashed against the side of his head. For a fraction of a second he blacked out. The leather-covered fist had bounced of his skull, rupturing a small vein at his temple. A headache started that Carter knew would last for hours.

It went on. He lost track of the blows. He heard the questions but he never opened his mouth.

". . . What is your name?"

". . . Who do you work for?"

". . . What are your orders?"

Carter's silence infuriated the colonel. The military man, not accustomed to losing this kind of battle, shouted his questions, took off his hat, wiped his brow, loosened his tunic, and finally spat at his captive in frustration.

The spittle ran down Carter's face, mixing with the

blood and sweat that dripped from his chin. the fluids landed on the soiled Khaki pants. They were all he'd been allowed to keep. He was barefoot in the cold cement room.

It was dark in his cell. He was cold. A light shone in a corridor around a corner giving off a faint glow that permitted him to see outlines of the objects in his cell.

His teeth were chattering. His head was one constant pain. He looked for something to cover himself and found a thin blanket. He curled into a fetal position on the straw mattress and started to think through his position.

He was still alive. So they wanted more from him. No one who appeared to be a foreign spy could be allowed to die until he had been sucked dry of information. And they had got nothing from him. Unless they resorted to drugs, they never would.

He sensed a scuffling noise to his right, about ten feet away. Rats. It was usually rats in a place like this.

"I heard them beat you, comrade," someone said. "Are you all right?"

Carter didn't answer at first. It was probably a plant. Then he realized he wasn't thinking, that the pain in his head was affecting his judgment. If it was a plant, he could clam up. If not a plant, then he might learn something.

"I'll live, comrade," he replied.

"Who are you?"

"Filip Andropov," Carter said. It was a Russian name he used when someone threw the question at him unexpectedly. It came to his lips naturally. "A sailor just in from Istanbul."

"Andropov? Not related to . . .?"

"No."

"What do they have you for?" the voice asked. It was weak. The man's age could be forty to seventy. He sounded old, but it could just be his condition.

"How do I know?" Carter answered. "I don't understand their questions. Goddamned KGB. It's the same all over."

"You're right, comrade. It's the same all over."

"Where is this place?" Carter ventured. "I was unconscious when they brought me here." He was probably in the house converted to a jail he'd seen earlier. But it didn't hurt to have the lay of the land.

"The jail. A house near their headquarters. They turned it into a jail. Damned butchers. They never change."

"What are you here for?" Carter asked.

"I'm called a dissident. One of my distinguished colleagues, a man who calls himself a scientist, turned me in out of jealousy."

"And what did you do?"

At first the man was silent. "I was foolish," he finally said. "They warned me in Moscow I would have no more chances." Again he stopped again but just for a moment. "I question authority. I tell inferior minds that they are inferior."

"Is that all?" Carter asked.

"It is enough when you have so much petty jealousy in the Academy of Science. The gulags are filled with . . ." He stopped, a sob breaking through the words, echoing around the cement walls.

"Is that where they are sending you?" Carter asked.

"It is what they threaten. They may do it this time. They may not. I have finished my project."

"I am a simple fisherman," Carter said. "I don't understand why the new buildings, why so many men of science."

"Our exalted General Secretary was born in this town, this end of the earth, a hole fit for the likes of him," the voice came back bitterly.

"Careful, comrade. That is dangerous talk."

"What the hell does it matter? I'm a dead man. I never did learn to keep my thoughts to myself."

"I understand, comrade. I feel the same but I keep it to myself. Tell me more about this place."

"A hole fit for peasants," the voice said with sarcasm. "Moscow is my home. But the state decides where you will live and work. The damned fool Morozov decides to give his hometown prosperity and the whole Academy of Science is moved here. The part that really contributes in any case."

"And who turned you in, comrade?"

"Boris Leonid Pivnev, the chief of staff here. A man who has never contributed one thing to science but who kisses ass in Moscow better than anyone else in the Academy. So he is the best man to be the director. Who else?"

Carter noted that the man's voice was weaker than when they started. He knew he'd better get what he could now. "Are there any others who feel as you do?" he asked.

"An interesting question, comrade. A question asked by someone they would plant to learn what they could not drag from me."

Carter laughed. The laughter rolled off the walls and bounced back at his throbbing head. Pain filled his eyes, his ears, his whole brain. He cut the laughter short. "My poor head," he said, laughing softly as he spoke. "I thought the same of you, comrade. It is the best joke I've heard in weeks."

"It is not funny, Andropov. I will never see her again. If I thought you would see her, be able to talk with her, I would tell you if there was another almost as foolish as I."

Carter thought about the statement for a minute. Someone, a woman, felt the same as this man. Maybe it was the woman Nadya Karpova. It would be true to the luck he'd been having on this job if the man with him was Filip Igor Pavlov.

"You haven't told me your name, comrade," he said.

"Filip Igor Pavlov at your service, comrade. A man of science but a fool."

"I have heard of you."

"A simple sailor has heard of Pavlov? I've never seen a Russian sailor who was interested in anything but the next woman he would lay," the weak voice said, a trace of humor in it despite the obvious pain.

"Electronics, aerodynamics, father of the Foxbat series," Carter recited from the file that Howard Schmidt had given him to read back at Dupont Circle.

"You know of my work?" Pavlov asked, amazed.

"Simple sailors sometimes surprise, Filip Igor. We share the same first name. The fates may have brought us together. Perhaps I can communicate with this woman for you."

"Perhaps. But how do you know you will ever see the outside of this place?"

Carter's voice held a timbre, a strength it had not before. "I will leave here, comrade. Be certain of that. I have been in worse places." He paused, then sat up with his back to the wall. "Your friend Chestyakov made it. He has been safe in the United States for about five weeks."

"You know Chestyakov? You saw him?"

"That's why I am here," Carter told the man. "He told me that Nadya and you would help."

The cell was silent for a few seconds while the man of science challenged his tired brain to think. "I believe you. Thank god Viktor got out, that one of us got out," he said, his voice weakening. "I have two broken legs," he told Carter. "Even if they intended this as a last warning, I could not work here for weeks. So I am finally useless to them." He stopped and took a few rasping breaths. The agony of unset bones came through his weakened speech as he forced himself to continue. "I'm also useless to you, Filip Andropov—or whoever you are."

"What about Nadya Karpova?" Carter asked.

"She will end up like me if someone doesn't help her. They have warned her once in Moscow," Pavlov said, his voice weakening with every statement he uttered. "Pivnev is probably looking for an excuse to get to her. He will go after her for himself, to satisfy his stupid lust, if she opens her mouth again. Then his shrew of a wife will take care of the rest. She's had other women sent to the gulags, women who were brilliant but who were trapped by Pivnev, the brainless, horny bastard they put in charge here. Oh, God! What the hell kind of a country was I born into? I wish I were dead!" he moaned.

Carter waited until the man regained his composure. He knew if he were in the scientist's position he would never have revealed the woman's name. But now he was sure the man was genuine and not a plant. He wished he could be sure the walls didn't have ears. What the hell? The colonel knew what he was. The danger was in implicating the woman before he ever got to her.

"I know you will help me, tell me where she is, only if you think if safe, Filip Igor," Carter finally said. He had to take the chance. "If you tell me where she is, give me some sign from you, I will take her out of this."

The man was sobbing out his misery now without trying to stifle his emotions. "God help me, I believe you. She must be saved. She must! Yes. Chestyakov . . . did not mislead you. Her name . . . is Nadya. Nadya Karpova. She is . . . the most brilliant computer scientist in this hellhole. A woman to be admired . . . and cherished."

"One other thing, Pavlov. Where does Pivnev live? And where can I find your Nadya?"

Carter waited a long time. He was sure the man had changed his mind.

"Tell her . . . I did it for her own good. Tell her I always loved . . . loved her . . . but I've been a fool all these years. Play the Cyrano . . . for me, Filip Andropov, and take her . . . take her a thousand miles from here."

Carter memorized the description of the house Pivnev occupied and the location of Nadya's apartment. He asked what Pavlov remembered of the jail they were in and was pleased to find the man had total recall. He described the basement and the first floor, everything he had seen, in minute detail.

Now was the time. Carter's energy level, normally exceptional, was at an all-time low. But he had to go on. This one was just too big for him to fail.

SIX

Night and day all seemed the same to Carter. The dim light around the corner from his cell still shone the same. Pavlov had not talked for hours. His mumblings became almost unintelligible and finally were replaced by irregular snoring. It was just as well. The man was about at the end of his rope and he'd given Carter all he could.

The layout of the house was simple. They had constructed three cells in the basement. The interrogation room was at the back of the house on the first floor. The colonel's office was next to the front entrance.

A guard visited twice a day to leave rancid food and to empty Carter's foul-smelling slop pail. He carried a battery lamp. The last time he'd visited, Carter saw his watch clearly, a military watch showing it was 2000 hours, eight o'clock at night. He had counted off the minutes since then. It was about nine-thirty, dark, a time when the sentries would be lax, thinking about their friends playing cards and drinking vodka.

"Pavlov!" he called out. "Wake up, Pavlov!"

"Wha . . ." the scientist mumbled groggily.

"It is time. I need your help."

56

"You picked the wrong man, Filip Andropov. I can do nothing for you."

"Listen to me, my friend. If you treasure your Nadya, you will concentrate. Are you with me?" Carter asked. He hated to risk his safety on the efforts of a man so close to the edge, but he had little choice.

"What can I do?" the weak voice finally responded.

"You will count to five hundred. Count to five hundred and then shout for the jailers. Tell them I am dead, that you heard my last breath."

"You're mad, Filip Andropov. But I will do it."

"Good. Start counting now," Carter said urgently.

The man from AXE lay back on the straw-filled sacking. He started taking great breaths and drew the air deep within his abdomen, yoga breathing, slow and deliberate. In a minute or two the breaths were very shallow, almost nonexistent. Then they seemed to disappear altogether.

The cell was cold. It had been cold from the beginning. Carter's skin was cold, his lips blue, his limbs rigid.

A loud wailing started in the cell near him. Pavlov was summoning up his reserves to put on a good show. "He's dead! Get him out of here! He's dead and he stinks already! Get him away from me!"

Soon the lamp shone along the hallway. Its light came around the corner. Pavlov kept up his wailing. The guard came to the bars, held up his lamp, and squinted to see into the back of the cell.

"Shut up, comrade! I can see for myself, can't I?" the guard shouted over the mournful wailing.

Filip Igor Pavlov stopped, his last cries bouncing off the walls, disappearing like smoke down a ventilating shaft.

All was quiet. The sound of the guard's feet, the scraping of leather on cement, was the only sound.

Carter was still, not moving a muscle, cold and still, almost in a state of trance. The guard was alone. He called

up the stairs but no one came. He fumbled with the keys
and came over to Carter's straw bed. He moved closer,
cautiously, inch by inch, bending over to check Carter's
chest for a heartbeat.

A hand snaked up and with the power of a vise squeezed
a grouping of nerves at the guard's neck. It was not enough
to kill him, but he'd be out for an hour or more.

The Killmaster lay still for a moment, recovering the
strength he had forfeited to the yoga trance and the hand grip.

Slowly he pushed off the guard and rose to his feet. He
moved across his cell to Pavlov. He could barely see the
man in the dim light. The scientist was curled up in a
corner, his legs at an odd angle.

"I can take you out of here if we move quickly," he
said.

"Go with God, whoever you are. And help my Nadya,"
Pavlov rasped in a voice filled with emotion. "Tell her I am
dead. It will be better."

Carter thanked the man for his help, then headed for the
stairs. He took them slowly, confidently, his strength re-
stored.

The ground floor was quiet. He padded barefoot to the
colonel's office. It was open. No one was around. He
opened the drawers of the desk and found nothing of interest. A clothes closet in one corner was partly open. He
eased open the door and found clothing of all kinds on
hangers. Only one item caught his eye. A suit of black
fatigues complete with webbing. He slipped off his filthy
pants and donned the black suit as quietly as possible. He
grabbed a black wool cowl and a pair of sturdy boots.

Still barefoot, he made his way to the back of the house.
The interrogation room was empty. It smelled of antiseptic
as if freshly cleaned.

Cupboards lined one wall, Carter hadn't seen them before. During the beating his back had been toward them.

He opened the doors one at a time and in the last one found his weapons. He smiled tightly as he strapped them on. He'd had Pierre all along but hadn't needed him. Wilhelmina's clip was full. Hugo was clean and shiny. They made him feel like a whole man again.

In a room close by, he heard snoring. It was a guardroom. The second guard slept soundly on a cot in a corner. He would never know how close he came to death. The Killmaster, now in charge of his own destiny, stopped to put on the battle boots and the cowl. A black wraith, one with the cloudless night, he crept through a rear door to freedom.

The Pivnev house was on Weilun Ulitsa, one street to the east of Red Square and the municipal building. It was a large house, one that had probably been requisitioned from a town official during the great migration from Moscow.

Carter was sure he had the right house when he saw a guard patrolling near the front door. None of the other houses on the street were as grand or had special protection. The guard seemed young and alert. He moved through a pattern that took him around the front of the house and part of the two sides. He was probably one of a pair.

It was past ten. Carter had no way of knowing how long the guards had been on duty or when they were relieved, but it didn't matter. He figured he would try to be in and out of the house with what he needed as quickly as possible.

The sky was cloudy and there was no moonlight. Carter waited until he had full night vision before he stalked the sentries.

A wall around the grounds was of red brick, the same as the house. It was about eight feet high. Carter scaled it and dropped to the soft ground inside while the sentry made a turn around the east side of the house.

As the Soviet guard returned to the front of the building, his Kalashnikov slung over his shoulder, Carter hit him a crushing blow with the butt end of his Luger. The man would be out for quite a while. That was three guards in a row whose life he had spared. He was getting downright humanitarian, he thought. The poor bastards deserved a better fate than a knife in their ribs in a remote town a thousand miles from home.

He eased the young giant into the bushes at the front of the house. Around back, another guard, a match for the first, paced as regularly as the other. They were like a set of wind-up toys.

The Killmaster was waiting for the guard to come to him, when he heard a vehicle approach from the direction of the square. He was in the process of ducking out of sight when headlights cast his shadow at the guard's feet.

The guard turned and unslung his weapon. The noise he made sliding his weapon's cocking lever was loud in the night as the sound of the vehicle faded.

Carter kept to the shadows as the guard advanced. He holstered his Luger, and Hugo slipped into his waiting palm. When the young guard was close enough, Carter lunged. The stiletto went up and in but glanced off a rib. The wound was not fatal. The guard could sound an alarm.

Instead of crying out, the guard reversed his rifle and swung it in an arc. It was the desperate move of a man in pain, fighting an unseen enemy. His action was stupid but lucky: the rifle butt caught Carter on the elbow, spinning Hugo into the bushes.

The Killmaster struggled to his feet and lunged at the figure in the dark. He knew he had no time for this, and caught the guard with a judo chop to the throat. The Russian went down instantly, his throat constricted, his last gasps loud in the silence of the night.

Suddenly the clouds parted and a new moon bathed the house in pure white light like a searchlight at a movie premiere. Carter scrambled through the bushes for a few seconds looking for his stiletto. The shiny blade reflected light for a fraction of a second, but it was enough. He slipped it into the chamois sheath on his arm and crept close to the shadows, out of the damning light.

All the windows on the ground floor were dark and locked. The front door was locked; the back door was not. A small room inside the door acted as a guardroom. It was equipped with a hot plate and coffee pot, and a small couch along one wall.

Carter made a complete recon of the three-story house. The Pivnevs slept in the master bedroom on the second floor. A couple, probably servants, slept on the third floor. It was barely more than a garret.

He crept up on the two sleeping figures, overpowering them one at a time with a pressure hold to nerve junctions at the side of their necks. When they were both helpless, he tore up a sheet and bound them, then returned to the floor below.

The Pivnevs slept in a giant bed. The moon provided enough light to show them stretched out naked, one arm of the wife across the back of the husband. He was a large man with huge buttocks and a roll of fat around his middle. He was bald except for a ring of black hair above his ears.

The woman was not much different. Running to fat, she had love handles where none were intended. Her mousy brown hair was cut very short. A blond wig was displayed on a Styrofoam mannequin head. It graced a cosmetic table at the other end of the room.

Carter turned on a soft light at the head of the bed and sat on a chair he had pulled up, his Luger in one hand.

"Boris Leonid Pivnev," he said close to the man's ear.

The man continued to snore, but the woman opened both eyes wide and sat up straight. Instead of screaming she just sat, the layers of fat making folds along her abdomen, her gaze riveted on the man in black seated near her husband.

"Who the hell are you?" she asked, her voice low and harsh.

"Wake up your husband," Carter commanded, waving his gun toward Pivnev. "You'll find out soon enough."

Instead of waking her husband, she snaked a gun from under her pillow and began firing while Carter brought Wilhelmina to bear.

He felt a red hot tearing of his flesh down low on his left side and another at his left shoulder before he saw her die. The top of her head disappeared, spread across the bedroom wall, as a 9mm slug from his Luger blew away flesh and bone.

Pivnev came awake with a start that threw Carter off the bed. Before he could react to the wounds and the fall, the fat man was on him, trying to wrestle the gun from his hand. Pivnev managed to knock the Luger from Carter's grip and was reaching for it.

The stiletto sprang into the Killmaster's hand. He wasted no time slipping the blade through layers of fat, between ribs, and to its target. He felt the man's hold relax and the body weight press down on him as the Russian scientist rolled on top of the wounded AXE agent.

Carter couldn't move the man's body off his own. It was as if he'd lost all his strength. He tried to push the dead weight from him as blackness closed in. He felt himself drowning in a sea of sticky red liquid as he spiraled over downward to a black void.

* * *

Colonel Nikolai Gladkov paced his office at KGB head-quarters three doors down the avenue from the house that was now a jail. He had seen the guard in the cell, sitting up and rubbing his neck. And when he'd pulled the surprise inspection he'd seen the other, the one who had been asleep in the back room.

Their prisoner was the most important captive Gladkov had taken in his whole career. The man had probably been sent to sabotage the new science building. At first the colonel's fury had known no bounds. He had ordered the two guards put in irons until he decided what to do with them. Later, as his temper cooled, he realized the escaped man had nowhere to go. The airport had a double ring of guards twenty-four hours a day. No boats had left the harbor. It was almost impossible to escape across the mountains that ringed the town. To be sure of no mountain escape, he'd ordered a squadron of helicopters to scour the slopes of the mountains north and east of town for some sign of the fugitive. They had seen nothing. No one had seen any-thing.

Gladkov panicked. This was his big chance and he wasn't about to blow it.

"I want the whole town searched!" he screamed at his officers as they trooped into his office. "I want every office and every house thoroughly searched right now, tonight! That bastard Andropov, or whoever he is, will not slip through my fingers again!"

Carter regained his senses and felt the suffocating weight lying across him. Panting, he pulled himself out from under Pivnev's corpse. As he struggled, a tearing pain pulled at his left flank and his left shoulder. When he stood up, feeling weak and dizzy, he examined his wounds care-fully. He had lost a lot of blood. The black fatigues were soaked all down the left side. He pulled them off and examined his wounds in the bathroom.

The wound in his flank had an entry and an exit. The slug left two small holes. The gun had been small-caliber. The other slug was still in his left shoulder.

Carter hid the black coveralls under an old-fashioned bathtub with claw feet. He tore a clean towel into strips and bound his wounds. A closet provided a black suit, too big but wearable. He slipped on the pants and jacket, made sure he had his weapons, and positioned Pivnev so he was over the pools of blood on the floor. Carter didn't want his pursuers to know right away that he was wounded.

The moon had retired to the cover of dense cloud banks again. The street was quiet. He walked quickly across the road, in great pain, to a wall surrounding a house that looked deserted. As he settled with his back against the bole of an old tree, a troop carrier entered the street and started a search of the buildings.

Carter crawled to the shadows inside the wall. The soldiers searched the house across the street first. When they found the guards and the dead couple all hell broke loose. Before they started a more thorough search, Carter slipped away, across Red Square to the new apartment buildings on Novoza Prospekt.

Nadya Karpova lived at 50 Novoza Prospekt, on the sixth floor, apartment 61. The building was only partially filled, and Pavlov told Carter that only one other apartment was occupied on the sixth floor.

The avenue was filled with troop carriers. Scores of soldiers swarmed through number 50, knocking on every door, searching every apartment. Carter sat in the shadows behind a massive oak tree, waiting. The searchers moved on to number 60. He kept to the shadows, found a rear door, and slipped into a deserted stairwell.

The stairs were dark. He checked to make sure he

wasn't bleeding through the toweling and leaving a trail. He wasn't, but the wounds throbbed. He needed medical help or he could come down with an infection. Carter cursed his situation. He had no time to be laid up, nowhere to seek medical help, and no time in any case.

He made it to the sixth floor. Every level from one to six was like scaling Mount Everest. When he got to the top, he was faint, barely able to stand. He doubted if he could go much farther. He was thankful that Nadya Karpova had an apartment to herself. He was glad that only one other resident was on this floor. But he didn't feel good about much else in this assignment.

He crept down the hall, barely able to keep from blacking out.

At the door to number 61, he rapped softly while leaning against the doorframe, his brain spinning.

The door opened. The face of an angel scowled out at him. "What the hell do you want now?" a voice said in anger. "You've searched —"

He lurched forward, fell to his knees, and sprawled out on the carpeting inside her door.

"Filip Pavlov says hello," was all he could get out before the black haze found him again.

Nadya Karpova closed the door and stood over the apparition that had just invaded her home. Her first thought was to call the men who had just searched her apartment, but the mention of Pavlov's name had stopped her. They had taken Filip days ago and she didn't know what they had done with him. Poor Filip, always spilling out his thoughts when he should keep them to himself.

And this one's face was battered as if he had been beaten. Careful, Nadya Karpova, she told herself. They have done this before. This one could be a plant, someone who had taken a beating to get close to her, to find out if she was another Pavlov.

The stranger lay on his back. Even with the bruises, she could tell that he was a good-looking man. The suit he wore was far too large. Then she noticed the blood seeping through the cloth from one shoulder and from his thigh.

She pulled open the jacket and saw the towel bandage. She eased it aside and saw a red and inflamed hole in his shoulder. It was close to a wound that had just healed. She bit her lip, knowing she couldn't afford to get into this. She was about to call for help when the handsome stranger spoke again.

"I have a message from Pavlov," he said through cracked lips. "Tell her I did it for her own good," he whispered. "Tell her I always loved her but I've been a fool all these years. Play the Cyrano for me, Filip Andropov, and take her a thousand miles from here."

She looked at him in amazement. The words seemed to come out as if burned into his brain. It was exactly what Filip Pavlov would have said if the reluctant Pavlov had suddenly gained the speech of love.

The stranger had passed out again. She put her arms under his shoulders and with surprising strength dragged him to her bed. With great difficulty she hoisted him from the floor.

The trousers came off with ease. He wore nothing underneath. Other than the suit jacket, he had nothing on but the strips of toweling . . . and the weapons.

This was insanity, she kept telling herself. She looked at the weapons, at the raw wounds, and the myriad scars on this powerful body, and she knew she was in for a rough time.

But the words he had uttered were so true to her friend Pavlov that she had to find out what happened to him.

Tell her I did it for her own good. He must have meant

sending this man to her was for her own good. But why? Was this one going to take her away from it all, from the serfdom she had suffered all her life? Since their friend Chestyakov had disappeared they had been caught between elation and despair. Was it possible to get out? Was Chestyakov alive or dead?

Tell her I always loved her but I've been a fool all these years. Poor Filip Igor. He had been a friend, a confidant. But he could never have been to her what he had dreamed. Oh, she knew what had been in his mind. But he had always been too shy and she hadn't encouraged him. Her actions had been calculated. He was not for her. They might have thought alike, but she would not be a fool as he had been a fool. She would bide her time. She would strike only when she had a chance for success. She would not spout her feelings for the sake of principles.

Play the Cyrano for me, Filip Andropov, and take her a thousand miles from here. So he had sent this one, Filip Andropov, a man also called Filip and with the name of the most dreaded man in the Soviet Union. Was he truly a savior—or a man like the one whose name he bore? Could he take her out of the hell that was her life? She had worked so hard. But for what? To be caged like an animal and ordered to use her talents for the state? That was not what she'd worked for through the years.

Was this one capable of taking her a thousand miles from here? If he was, then he was not one of them. He was from a place a thousand miles from here. And it wasn't Moscow. She had a good brain and she knew how to use it. This man was not one of them at all. He was probably not even a Russian.

So who was he?

SEVEN

The room was small, a studio apartment setup, everything in one room plus a bathroom. Carter was in a double bed, slightly groggy but feeling surprisingly well. His wounds were expertly bandaged. The other side of the bed was warm and still bore the imprint of her body.

She walked slowly from the bathroom, combing her long dark hair. As she used both arms to wield the brush and fluff out the sparkling strands, her elbows bent outward and her breasts moved sensuously.

She was clothed only in a thin nightgown. She had the kind of body that caused men to suck in their guts and parade like peacocks in front of women, doing ritual dances of courtship like wildfowl. She was tall, about five feet nine, and she carried herself with a dancer's grace. Her complexion was perfect, her teeth white and even, her eyes a pale blue, almost white.

Finished with her brushing, she coiled her hair into a knot at the back and anchored it with a few hairpins and combs. She slipped into plain panties and a cotton bra. Her blouse was white and cut severely with no frills. The tailored suit she donned was a bit too big, as if she wanted to hide the delights underneath. Her shoes were low-heeled pumps, designed more for comfort than style. The horn-rimmed glasses she slipped on helped transform her into a plain Jane, a woman neither particularly pretty nor just someone who would be unnoticed in a crowd.

She was suddenly aware of his scrutiny. She moved to the bed and knelt to his level. "You've been watching me," she said casually, in remarkably good English.

"My morning eye-opener," he said in Russian. "You are a beautiful woman, Nadya Karpova. It is fortunate the bathroom is too small for dressing. It was a privilege to share your morning routine," he added, grinning.

"I have to report to the lab," she said, also slipping into Russian. "I'll make an excuse, feign illness, and be back in three or four hours."

"You fixed my wounds. I feel much stronger. How did you . . . ?"

"A long story, Filip Andropov, if that is your name. I was a medical student, almost passed my exams. They decided I was a better research scientist.

"Do not use water while I am gone. The floor wardens will hear the flow in the pipes. The kettle is full. You can plug it in and make coffee or tea," she said, rising to her full height, standing over him. "I don't have to tell you to move around quietly."

"One thing," he said, holding up a hand to delay her. "Why? I appear to have your confidence. I barely spoke to you last night."

"But you said the magic words," she said. "Filip Pavlov is dear to me. He was one of the few honest men I knew." She moved down to his level again, looked him in the eye. "I wasn't in love with him. He was just a good man, a man who thought as I. He wouldn't have opened up to you if he didn't know, deep down, you could help me."

"What else?" he asked, knowing she was holding back.

"He's dead, isn't he," she said, tears forming in her eyes.

Carter thought of Pavlov's words—*Tell her I'm dead*—but he decided to tell her the truth. With this one it would always be the truth.

"He told me to tell you he was dead. He wouldn't let me take him out. He knew he would be a burden. Both his legs were broken and unattended."

"What do you think will happen to him?" she asked, the tears flowing.

Again the truth. "I think he is dead now," he said.

She rose again and headed for the door, wiping her eyes with the back of her hand. "I will be back soon," she said as she reached for the door.

"Wait," he said. "There is something else you should know."

"What is it?" she asked, coming closer, standing over him.

"Chestyakov sent me," he said simply.

She dropped to her knees, her face close to his. "Viktor Mikhailovich? How do you know him? Who are you, really?" she asked intently, her hands on his shoulders.

Carter winced as she continued to grasp him. She relaxed her grip. "He has been in the United States for weeks," he told her. "He told me about you."

"You are American?" she asked, her beautiful ice-blue eyes wide, the surprise delaying the next question for a minute. "What do you think you can do?"

"When I'm feeling stronger I have work to do here. Then we will leave together."

"I've prayed for this . . . but now . . . when it is close, I'm not sure."

"Don't weaken now, Nadya. You still feel the same way. Chestyakov made it and you will make it."

She rose and headed for the door again. "I will be back as soon as I can," she said.

He lay in the bed, the covers pulled up to ward off the chills. He was stronger but he was not yet strong enough to tackle the work he had to do. He had been lucky to run into Pavlov and even luckier to have found Nadya. You could never be sure about the Chestyakovs of this world.

As sleep claimed him again he was thinking about what lay ahead. He'd promised to take her out with him and that could be a difficult promise to keep.

Carter's eyes fluttered open to find two of the most beautiful eyes he'd ever seen looking into his from only two feet away. She had removed her glasses and let her hair down. Her smile was warm and concerned.

"How do you feel?" she asked.

He stretched. Miraculously, he felt little pain. "I feel great, just great," he told her. "The shoulder . . . the bullet? It's been removed, hasn't it."

"It was as difficult as you think," she said, taking his hands. "It was a clean wound. The bullet was resting against the skin of your back. A simple slit and it was out."

"You make it sound simple."

"I wanted to be a surgeon. I was good. They let me do small operations when I was still a senior student and then they took it away from me."

"You've mentioned that twice. It sounds like a major disappointment," he said.

The almost white eyes looked at him. He felt he was being drawn deep into their depths.

"It has been my experience since I was sixteen or seventeen. They found I had an IQ of a hundred and ninety. They let me work in medicine to mature and develop. Then they snatched it from me, told me I was of more value to the state as a scientist."

"From what Pavlov told me, they were right."

"Poor Filip. He was a fighter without armor. Yes. He knew me well," she said bitterly, looking away for a moment. "I have hated every minute of it. I have hated being manipulated. You can't imagine how it feels to have no freedom in your whole adult life." She paused before continuing. "People from the West think we can't imagine what freedom would be like. Maybe they are right. But I have my own version of freedom," she said, her voice strong. "In the West I would be a surgeon and a good one. I would have a beautiful apartment where there would be no floor monitors watching all the time. I could travel when and where I wanted. I could buy the things I wanted, clothes, food, a car. These things are all imaginary now, but they are vivid, almost real in my dreams."

Carter took one of her hands in his. "You are a woman of great worth, Nadya Karpova," he said.

She drew her hand away and looked into his eyes for a full minute, searching for her own truth. Then she moved closer, tentatively, and pressed her lips to his.

Carter went with her, kept to her pace. He claimed her lips in a long kiss.

She was wearing a flannel robe. To his surprise, she shucked it off and slipped in beside him. They held each other, each needing comfort. Carter was still not strong enough to carry out his mission. Nadya was not strong enough to break away on her own. But Carter had a feeling that, given time, they would make a good team.

As the thought occurred, he felt her even breathing against his cheek. The tension she had been keeping under control had loosed within the warmth of their nest, with the stroking of his hand along her flank.

She was asleep. He continued to caress her gently, run-

ning his hand up and down her back and thighs until his
eyelids drooped and he too dropped off.

Gladkov sat in his office at the jail, snapping his baton
against his thigh like a metronome as he spoke. Each sentence was punctuated by the sound of leather striking cloth.

"He managed to get clear away from all of you."
Whack!

"You are a bunch of incompetents." *Whack!*

"You will all suffer for this." *Whack!*

"We have searched all the buildings in the old town,
Colonel," one of his officers offered. "Perhaps we should
search the rest of the town."

"You idiots!" he screamed at them, his baton crashing
down on the desk. "Of course we should search the rest of
the town! We should search all the boats, comb the lower
slopes of the mountains again, look in every nook and
cranny of all our official buildings."

"He might be posing as one of us," one of the men
offered.

"Then you damned well better check every one of our
people!" he raged.

"I looked over the scene at the Pivnev house," one of
the officers said. "Pivnev's wife fired three shots from a
pistol. We can find only one spent bullet in the room. It is
my belief that this man was hit twice."

Gladkov smiled for the first time. "Ah-hah! That's the
kind of news I want to hear!" he exclaimed. "Scour the
town for anyone with medical skills. Find out who treated
him. Start looking in the alleys and the foothills for a dead
body."

They all stood at attention, waiting for further orders,
cold sweat rolling down their backs under their tunics.

"Get the hell out of here!" he screamed at them. "Find something!"

Nadya stirred in his arms only minutes after his eyes opened. She had snuggled against him as she slept. He held her closely, tenderly, breathing in the smell of her hair, glorying in the heat of her, aroused by the feel of her skin against his.

She lifted her lips to his and clung to him, shivering slightly.

Carter held her gently, stroking her back and buttocks, talking to her softly. Gradually he let his fingers drift to her flat stomach and below. She moaned as he touched her, and pressed herself against his hand.

When he was ready, he gently positioned her above him and moved to her. He felt her tense as he entered her. He stayed still, kissing her neck, reassuring her, feeling the heat of her build, remaining motionless until he felt her body raise slightly, only then beginning to move with her.

They built up the tempo, Nadya moaning softly in his ear. He had the feeling that she wanted to cry out, but he knew she wouldn't. The walls were like paper.

He felt himself ready to explode, and the heat within her was like a furnace. Her moaning picked up in tempo. When she was almost at her peak he took over, playing her like a priceless instrument, taking her to the heights, to a performance she would remember always, to the joys of exquisite delay.

And when they could hold off no longer, their bodies shuddered their pleasure in unison, both of them straining to make it last for as long as possible.

Then it was over and she lay on him, her chest heaving, her perfect breasts rising and falling as they both coasted down the long slope from ecstasy to reality.

"That was wonderful," she whispered.

Carter smiled and held her tight. He lay content. As he gradually came back to normalcy, a question that had haunted him had to be asked.

"Earlier today, your first words to me were in English," he said. "Why?"

The answer was a long time in coming. She rolled to one side and rested on an elbow, the incredible ice-blue eyes boring into his.

"Because you are American," she said.

"How did you know?"

"I guessed you were not Russian, so what were you?" she said. "While I was taking care of you, I couldn't help but see all your scars. And I found your weapons. From those clues I decided you must be a spy. I guessed an American spy." She grinned. "Not very scientific decision-making, I admit, but I was right."

"Where did you learn to speak English?"

"At one time they thought I'd serve them best as a spy, doing scientific espionage. Even back then I think they were able to see my tendency to criticize and even defect."

"Has it been with you that long, this feeling?" he asked, stroking the hair back from her face.

"Ten years. Maybe fifteen. I'm a thirty-year-old mal-content," she said wryly. "Always complaining."

"So what did you think an American was doing here? Before I told you about Chestyakov, that is," he asked, almost afraid to hear the answer.

"Only one possible answer. You came in answer to my prayers," she said, laughing.

He waited, looking into those beautiful eyes until she turned serious.

"You've come to destroy our files," she said simply.

"Is that what comes from having a genius IQ?" he asked.

"I'm sure our dear Colonel Gladkov, whose IQ may be

three digits but I sincerely doubt it, has figured it out. You don't have to be a genius."

"So everyone here will be pitted against the attempt."

"Right. But they don't know you have me on your side. Doesn't that change the odds?" she asked.

"It does indeed."

"Just what is it you came for, exactly?"

This was the moment of truth. Carter had decided earlier to be straight with her, but this was the acid test.

"It's a tough job. I must select some of the most recent scientific developments and send them back to my people by modem, then destroy as much of the rest as I can," he said.

"You don't mess around, do you? Who will pick up the modem signal?" she asked.

"I don't know yet. I'll have to contact my people about that. But first I want to see the inside of the new building. I've got to see the setup for myself. I want to select the best place for charges after we've sent out the modem stuff."

"Explosives? Why bother? There's a better way to destroy magnetic tape."

"Like what?" he asked.

"Why not degauss them?" she asked. "There's got to be some way to wipe all of them clean."

"It's a good idea, but I've heard that some experts can restore demagnetized tapes."

She looked at him and gave him her most dazzling smile. "Don't believe it," she said. "If we could find some large magnets and drive them up and down the aisles for an hour or two, that would do the job."

"Sure. I'll find some big magnets, put them on poles, sling them on my shoulders, and roller skate up and down the aisles, " he said, starting a low laugh.

"Or you could wrap a few coils of copper wire around

the building and put just the right charge through them and we'd have a giant electromagnet. All the tapes would be in one giant magnetic field. They'd be as clean as when they left the factory."

"Sure. We'll get Superman to fly around the building and coil the wire. Then we'll find some large generators to connect the wire to. No sweat." He shook his head and chuckled, then got serious again.

"What about the modem work?" he asked. "What's worth our while?"

"Did you know we are much further advanced in SDI than your people?" she asked. "We have the technology to send lasers into space and cover the whole tracking system between our two countries. Another year and we'll have the first one on space."

He whistled softly. "What other gems do you have?"

"Some of my work. Artificial intelligence that will robotize our industries. In ten years we can outstrip you in production," she said, obviously proud of her accomplishments.

"What about military hardware?" he asked.

"A new Foxbat series that makes our current Foxbat MIG 32 series look like toys. Better than your best F-16s by maybe twenty percent," she said, her face grave, her mind actively making the choices. "A plan for a new atomic missile cruiser that will be built of alloys stronger than steel. It has built-in force fields to repel your missiles, speeds to compare with hydroplanes."

"How long will all this take to send by modem?" he asked.

"They're all on separate tape reels," she said. "If I could put them all on one, maybe it could go out by high-speed modem in a half hour. Why not a separate reel to take home as insurance?"

"Won't that be dangerous for you to arrange?" he asked, his brow furrowed.

"Not really. I have access to it all, highest priority. I can make two tapes and hide them in the building. I might be able to set up a modem where they can't find it and we can let it run while we try to degauss the reels."

Carter thought about this earlier prediction. He was right: he and Nadya Karpova would make a magnificent team. As if she read his mind, she clung to him, began to kiss his mouth and his whole face.

"Together, my American spy, we can do anything." And she smiled up at him, reached for him, and their bodies joined once again.

EIGHT

Nadya Karpova walked from her apartment building to the new science building in the rain. She wore a plastic raincoat and carried an umbrella. She was one of hundreds arriving at the same time, nodding casually to most, exchanging friendly greetings with a few.

This was going to be a trying day. She worried about the American back at her apartment and was concerned about her role that started right now, as soon as she was settled into her small office.

She rode the crowded elevator to the fifth floor. Her office was one of many along a solid wall in the middle of the building. In the Soviet, brilliance didn't necessarily warrant fine surroundings. She was a slave of the state. The fact that she was the star of the team didn't give her many privileges. It was one of the things that made her what she was. She had not swallowed the party line, though it had been fed to her since birth. Something in her rebelled, told her there was something better, told her it would come if she was patient.

Viktor Chestyakov and Filip Pavlov had been the only ones she had been able to discuss her feelings with recently. And before them a succession of men and women who had long since gone to the gulags, or worse, to a painful death in the cellars of a KGB prison. Each disappearance and each death had strengthened her resolve. She had been the only one who had kept her feelings to herself. Of those who died or disappeared, none had never uttered her name. So, as far as she knew, she was still clean, considered a loyal party worker willing to give her talent and her genius to the cause forever, and for little gain.

She thought about this for the first few minutes she sat at her desk. They had been wrong. All the party chiefs she had met who had complimented her on her work, all the men and women who had supervised her projects, lesser brains than hers, party hacks—they had all been wrong. She was a bomb about to explode. And she had kept it to herself. Unlike her friends who had ended up in trouble, she didn't need to rant at officialdom, to be labeled dissident, to be dragged out of her bed to be questioned and tortured. It was enough that the flame of freedom burned in her soul and she was aware of it every waking moment.

She shook herself. It was time to get to work. Her boss was in Moscow at a party conference. He wouldn't bother her for a week. Even when he was here he didn't interfere with her work. He waited, like most department heads, for her to finish a project, then he would present the results and take the credit.

She made a mental list of the tape reels she would need. Like Carter, she had total recall. She would leave no incriminating notes behind.

Her thoughts organized, she picked up a battered briefcase and headed for the ground floor that was the main storage area for computer tape reels.

She signed in at the door. Her status gave her unchallenged clearance. She sat at a terminal, called in the inventory, and made a small computer file of the references that interested her. They were printed out in seconds on a high-speed laser printer.

With her briefcase held like a shopping bag and the printout her shopping list, she walked up and down each aisle selecting one reel after another until she had a half dozen. She was lucky. With most of the department heads in Moscow, it was not a busy time at the Academy; none of the files she wanted were signed out.

Nadya attracted no attention. She was where she should be, doing nothing unusual. Now the difficult part would begin. She had never used the tape reel duplicator to any extent.

The room was almost empty. One other woman, a scientist she knew, was working at another of the huge duplicator machines.

Nadya selected the first reel from her case, snapped it onto the right-hand drive, and put a blank tape reel on the left. A keyboard allowed her to bring up the beginning of a file. It was the new Foxbat data on the live reel. She flipped three switches, and the machine began to duplicate the data from a designated start point to the end of that file.

The process took more than five minutes. While she waited, she thought about what she was doing. This file alone would allow the Americans access to every aspect of the most devastating fighter plane in the world. Her people had worked on it for years. It was the culmination of millions of hours of aeronautical and electronic achievement by thousands of scientists, including her.

The thought didn't dissuade her. She pulled the tape from the drive, replaced it with another, and continued her job.

"What are you doing, Comrade Karpova?" a deep voice behind her asked.

She turned quickly, her heart racing. It was a handsome young captain of the security guard. She knew him. He had taken an interest in her from time to time.

"I'm combining several projects onto one tape," she said, trying to keep the panic from her voice. "Saves me carrying a whole briefcase of them to my office. And the originals will still be available to others if I don't take them out of circulation."

"There's a regulation about that, comrade," he said. "You'd better come with me." He took her arm and started to pull her from the chair.

"Didn't you know, Captain? The policy's been changed," she lied. "If I sign out the new tape reel with a description of what is on it, the librarian will keep it on file and will degauss it when I am finished with it."

"Be sure you follow the new rule," he warned her. "And maybe you will have dinner with me tonight?"

She smiled at him, trying to look calm. She knew that beneath her suit jacket her blouse was plastered to her skin. "Sorry," she said. "My boss loaded me with work when he took off for Moscow. Maybe next week when he's back."

"I'll hold you to that, comrade. Next week," he said as he turned and left the room.

Her hands shook as she removed the reel that had been copied. In a few more minutes she would have it all, the Foxbat, the Soviet equivalent of SDI, the artificial intelligence, the robotry . . . all of it. The plan was to make a duplicate of the new reel, sign out the new reel, and hide the copy in the modem facility.

While she walked to the librarian's desk, she thought about the American and what they were going to do. He had gone over the plan with her and was apprehensive about her safety, but she had assured him she could do it. Somehow she had to find suitable clothes for them to make a night reconnaissance of the facility. So far she'd found two black turtleneck sweaters and some pairs of dark gloves.

At the desk she signed out the new tape reel, describing

what was on it. The librarian ran it through a reader at her desk to confirm the contents. She didn't check Nadya's case where the copy rested under a pile of file folders.

Free from the scrutiny of the file room, Nadya made her way to the computer room on the second floor and a separate room set aside for modem transmission.

The room was empty. Again the fact that their supervisors were in Moscow helped her cause. Everyone was lying down on the job, even the guards. She sat at one of the modems, looked around the room, and chose a file cabinet as her hiding place. The drawers didn't have locks. They contained bulging cardboard folders and obsolete reels long since struck from the list of classified records. She wrapped her duplicate tape in a plastic sleeve and shoved it in the back of the drawer. She used a marker pen to scrawl a name on it. She called it Filip in honor of the extraordinary man who had entered her life.

Carter was restless back at the apartment. Nadya had removed his bandages and decided to leave them open to the air. She used a new salve recently developed at the Academy. The bullet holes were starting to pucker and scab over already. He felt good.

The sound of motor vehicles caught his attention. Cautiously, he looked out the window that faced the street.

Police on their way to make yet another search.

Carter looked around the room quickly. Nadya had made the bed and washed the dishes. He pulled on his clothes, strapped on his weapons, and scanned the room for a telltale sign of his presence, but he found none. Nadya had even disposed of his bandages in the incinerator.

He opened the door a crack and heard voices on the floor below. He snapped the safety catch on the door so it wouldn't lock and headed for the roof. A ladder led to a skylight at the end of the hall. He scaled the ladder, pushed open the skylight, and climbed out onto the roof.

The wound on his shoulder broke open and started to bleed. He took off his shirt and tied it around the shoulder, stopping the flow.

The roof was like all the others on the apartment buildings around it. He could see police on some of the other roofs, but they didn't see him. Each roof was cluttered with heating units and massive ventilating fans. Some of them had cowls six feet across.

He unscrewed the nuts holding the cowl on one of the giant fans. He tipped the cowl sideways and crawled under it. It was like a giant mushroom head. He lay still, his nose inches from a fan with blades like scythes.

By craning his neck, Carter could see part of the roof. He waited, cramped as he was, for a full ten minutes. The roof door opened. Two men in khaki uniforms walked casually out into the bright morning sun. They shielded their eyes, looking his way.

He pulled his head in, curled up in a fetal position, and waited, his hand on the butt of his gun.

The crunch of gravel could be heard to the right and left. Carter could hear boots walk close to his hiding place and move on. He waited what seemed like hours until he could no longer hear their boots on the gravel, only the wind whistling up through the cowl and the blades of the fan.

He waited a few more minutes, then lifted the loose cowl and looked out at the roof. He saw no one, and eased himself to the roof. The police had deserted the other roofs. He walked to the parapets and looked down. They were getting into their trucks and moving on to another part of the town.

As he headed for the roof door, the blades of the fan started to whirl, building up to a crescendo that shook the roof. He laughed. Timing, he told himself. Timing was everything.

Gladkov's nerves reacted when the telephone rang. He snapped to attention in his chair. Some inner sense warned him that this was the call he dreaded.

"The General Secretary tells me you've been having some trouble down there," the director of the KGB snapped without waiting for a greeting. "Why the hell do I have to find out from him?"

"I didn't want to bother you with minor details, Comrade Director," Gladkov said, trying to keep his voice steady.

"I knew I should have entrusted the job to a younger man. All right, give it to me straight. What's he so excited about?"

"We've had a penetration, Comrade Director. No harm done. The man or group has been discouraged by my people. The danger is over."

"And what makes you think so?" the director asked with obvious sarcasm.

"We've searched every building in town and scoured the hillsides," Gladkov said. "Obviously my people were too much for him."

"Then search them twice."

"We've done that. Believe me, the danger is over, comrade."

"That's not what the General Secretary tells me. You had him in jail. He escaped. He left some guards disabled and some were killed. And you haven't found him—alive or dead. It doesn't sound like it's over to me," the director barked into the phone.

"We can handle it, Comrade Director. You can count on me."

"The General Secretary doesn't think so. He's sending a

force of *Spetslnaya Naznacheniya* as soon as they can be airborne."

A troop of the Spetsnaz were coming to Sukhumi? The crack special forces of the Red Army? Gladkov choked back his response. He knew it would be useless to complain. If the General Secretary ordered it, there was no way his boss could stop it.

"Do you know what this means?" the director screamed into the phone. "It means the army will have their big noses where we should have exclusive jurisdiction. The GRU— those clowns in army intelligence—will control them, Gladkov, you idiot. You've managed to accomplish what I've tried to avoid since taking office. My worst rival will have a foothold in the General Secretary's prize project!"

"The GRU . . . I'm sorry . . . we really thought—"

"It's too late to be sorry, you old fool!" the director cut in. "I'm going to keep you there. You know why? I wouldn't humiliate one of my other field commanders with the ignominy of working with the GRU."

"But we have cleaned up the situation, Comrade Director. There is no need to send—"

"It's done, Gladkov. It's out of my hands," the director said, his voice less shrill but his nerves still on end. "Prepare for them and keep our department in control. Do you hear? Keep the KGB in control of the situation."

"Yes, sir."

"Because if you don't . . ."

Gladkov didn't have to hear the rest. He'd sent too many men to the gulags himself. Strange, he thought, the fear gone for a second or two, you never thought it could happen to you. To someone else, sure, but never to you.

The bed seemed like a second home to Carter. The wounds were healing. He had regained his strength. Nadya had done as much as she could at the Academy building. It was up to him now.

On his third day with her, Nadya brought home a dial telephone, a local directory, and a coil of wire. After a supper of red cabbage and sausage patties, Carter went to work.

A telephone terminal box was located across the hall from the apartment door. Nadya didn't have telephone service, but some of the cable in the terminal box might be alive. The other tenant on the floor was home and cooking supper. Carter slipped outside and tested the terminals. Some were in use. He listened to the conversations and found they were routine.

Finally he found a live pair of wires that produced a dial tone when he connected the phone.

"Won't they be able to trace your call?" she asked, her beautiful eyes open wide.

Carter smiled at her. "I've studied the directory you brought," he told her. "The town has the most modern equipment available. I should be able to dial anywhere in the world."

"But they can hear you! They can listen in on anyone!"

He knew this was typical Russian paranoia and he had to reassure her. "This is electronic equipment," he explained. "They can't monitor all calls. They have to plan in advance to know we are making unauthorized calls. No one knows we are using this line."

He dialed in the numbers that took him to Washington and the computer Hawk had added to supervise AXE's communications a few years ago. A honeyed voice answered his code with a suggestive tone.

"Hi, Nicky," the voice purred. "What can I do for you?"

Nadya, her ear close to the phone, glared at him and asked suspiciously, "Who is that?"

He laughed. "You of all people should be able to recognize a synthesized voice." Nadya grinned sheepishly.

"The codes told you I wanted Hawk right away," he commanded the computer. "Get him."

"Nick," the gruff voice of the older man came on the line immediately. "How's it going?"

He told the head man of AXF about his meeting Filip Pavlov in jail and his finding Nadya. He made her sound like a miracle woman and implied that the scientific community could not do without her. He outlined her progress to date and the plans they had made. "She will transmit the most important data by modem to you. And I'm bringing her out with me, sir. She's more than earned it for what she's risked so far and what she'll do."

"Just be careful," Hawk sighed.

"How do we transmit the data?" Carter asked. "Do you have a receiver and a time frame?"

"The carrier *Ticonderoga* will be in your range. She's supposed to return to the Greek islands tomorrow."

"Have them start scanning at midnight tomorrow and for the next four nights. Keep them on-line until six each morning."

"You've got it. The woman has a wireless modem?"

"They seem to have everything at the new facility."

"How are you actually going to do it?" Hawk asked.

"I'm not sure yet, but I've got several ideas. I might need some help on this one," he admitted.

"Name it."

"If I need someone, I'll call you in a couple of days."

"Anything else?"

"Yes. Starting tomorrow night, have a helicopter rescue team scanning the Black Sea waters five miles out of the Bosporus. I can't think of any other route home from here."

"I'll arrange it. And, Nick, take care, you hear?"

"It sounds like you are well organized, Nick Carter," Nadya said to him after he'd hung up.

"I've never told you my real name," he said, holding

her away from him, looking into the now familiar ice-blue eyes.

"Nick Carter, AXE Killmaster, designated N3 with authorization to kill at your own discretion," she went on, a sly grin on her face.

He shook her, deadly serious now. "What the hell do you know about me?" he said in a whisper that commanded her attention. "How did you find out?"

She eased his hands from her shoulders, a laugh starting from her beautiful throat. "I told you they started to train me as a spy," she said. "You have locked horns with too many of our top people to be anonymous. You were a case study of the ultimate agent. They tried to make us in your image. We had no godhead to follow from the KGB or the GRU, so they used you."

He was speechless for a moment, drinking in what she said.

She laughed and pulled his face down to kiss him. She curled her fingers through his dark hair. "I'm flattered that I have the best to take me out. Now I know I'll make it. And we'll give your people enough to please them. Maybe the intelligence coup of the century."

He flopped on the bed and thought about what she'd said. He could give her no guarantees. He wasn't infallible no matter what they had taught her.

NINE

The next night she came home from the Academy to find him in a yoga position. It was almost the last of the twenty-six stretching exercises he practiced whenever he could. With her ministrations and the new drugs she'd used, his wounds had healed faster than he'd expected. All his muscles responded well, not without some stiffness but with enough tone to get him through almost any action.

Carter sat cross-legged on a small rug, dressed only in his shorts. He smiled up at her. "We go in tonight," he said. "Are you all set at your end?"

"Tonight? So soon? I thought . . ."

"We can look over the possibility of explosives and you can work on the modem," he said, looking up at her. "Any problems with that?"

"I just hadn't thought it would be so soon. We'll soon be out of here and I won't see you again."

He took her in his arms when she dropped her parcels and came to him on the rug. His thoughts were torn from the night's work as he held her in his arms.

His mind shifted gears again when he felt her hand slipping into his shorts and her mouth covering his. She had become voracious since that first day. He ground his lips to hers while starting on the buttons of her blouse . . .

Close to midnight they stood together examining the last details of their appearance. The black turtlenecks had been supplemented by dark blue coveralls, black canvas shoes, dark socks, and black wool stevedore caps. Nadya had found some black grease that they used to darken their faces. They each had black gloves. It was all makeshift but it would work. Carter had gone into worse situations with less camouflage. He wore his Luger harness over the sweater, and Hugo was snapped to his right forearm. Pierre was still taped high on his left thigh but was difficult to get at. He rationalized that he probably wouldn't need the small gas bomb.

"How far did you get in spy school?" he asked. "Did they teach you to handle weapons?"

"I can take care of myself. Don't worry."

But Carter did worry. He didn't know what they were going to run into. He didn't kill gratuitously, but he didn't hesitate whenever it was absolutely necessary, and in his work that was all too often. He would avoid it tonight if he could. He didn't want more waves of search teams prowling the streets, but he'd do what he had to.

Carter's prime concern was Nadya having to face reality. It was one thing for her to fantasize being taken to the West by her hero, and another to see the blood and violence that were part of the process. Okay. He couldn't do anything but press ahead. He'd find out soon enough if she could handle herself.

He led the way, taking the stairwell instead of the elevator. At the ground floor he took the back door leading to a grassy area surrounded by apartment buildings on most of three sides and the huge Academy building on the other.

The area was almost deserted. Three couples were sitting on blankets too absorbed in each other to notice two almost invisible figures make their way along one wall to the science building.

"How many guards are on the ground floor at night?" he whispered when they reached a back door.

"Not more than two," she said, her mouth close to his ear. "They're not very active. They keep mostly to the front of the building."

"I presume they have the usual surveillance cameras on each floor?" he asked as he examined the back door for alarms.

She nodded. "They were installed last month. But I don't think all of them are working yet."

The back door was not fitted with an alarm. Carter couldn't understand such sloppy security, but he didn't complain. He worked on the lock for almost a minute before he felt it respond to his tools.

They slipped inside. It was a back corridor, dimly lighted. A camera was pointed directly at them from the far corner. Carter walked up to it boldly. If it was working, they'd have been spotted already. It was stationary on its mount. They might be in luck after all. This was not like the Soviets he had dealt with before. There was too much laxity for so important an installation. But again, it was a situation he'd take advantage of.

Carter led the way to a stairwell. "I want to see the modem setup," he whispered. "You lead, but get the hell out of the way if we run into anyone."

Nadya took the stairs two at a time to a second-floor landing, unexpectedly opening up a gap between them. She opened a door and was in the corridor before the surprised Killmaster caught up to her.

As the door was starting to close in front of him, he heard a scuffle in the corridor. He rushed inside, Hugo in his right hand, to see a guard on the ground, clutching his throat and Nadya making a miraculous catch of his machine pistol just before it hit the ground.

The guard writhed on the tile floor, his mouth working furiously as his face turned a bluish red, his crushed windpipe robbing him of life.

Carter stood for a moment, staring at the scene. His questions about Nadya's competence in action had been answered, but now they had a dead man on their hands.

He decided they would have to part company for a few minutes. He gave her the call signal for the *Ticonderoga*'s communications room. "Get to the modem room while I get rid of him. Set up the tape reel and send it as soon as you get confirmation from the carrier. Any problems?" he asked.

She was standing, shaking, looking up at him, her eyes wide and frightened. "I've . . . known how to kill . . . to use some weapons . . . since the school. But I've never really killed."

He held her for a minute. She stopped shaking. "I'll be all right now," she said finally. "It was just, you know, the first. A human life."

She pulled herself free, tucked a strand of raven hair under her knit cap, and headed for an inner door. She took the machine pistol with her.

Carter hoisted the dead guard, feeling the shoulder wound complain for the first time in many hours. He took stairwell down to the basement and found a storage area that was filled with dust-covered boxes and obviously seldom used. He dumped the guard in an empty box and closed the lid. He thought of using the guard's uniform but discarded the idea. He didn't want his own inexperienced partner filling him full of 9mm slugs.

His job tonight was to learn the layout of the building and decide how to destroy the tape reels. If he knew where they had an ammunition dump, he might steal enough plastique to do the job, but that was a long shot.

As he walked the long rows of shelves, all filled with tape reels, he realized the job was much bigger than he thought. Each aisle ran almost the length of the building, close to a hundred yards, and each of the twenty aisles had a dozen rows of shelves on each side. At his best guess, they had to have thousands of tapes stored here.

He found the guardroom close to the front entrance. One man sat, his feet up, in front of a dozen screens, all dark. Nadya had been right. They hadn't been able to get the security system up yet. He couldn't believe it. At such a facility in the States, they'd either have it up and working or a guard at every aisle. The Soviets were usually paranoid about security. Something was definitely wrong in this command.

Before he caught up with Nadya, he made a complete survey of every floor. On the sixth, in a huge maintenance room taking up one whole corner of the building, he found three huge rolls of copper wire. In two crates, unopened, they had two high-voltage electric generators, probably to set up as an emergency power source. Beside them, ten-gallon drums of fuel waited to be pumped into their gasoline power plants. He found no explosives.

A plan was beginning to take form in his agile mind. Maybe one of Nadya's earlier ideas when they'd been kidding around wasn't so farfetched after all. It meant the need for a few hours in the building alone, without any interference. That would take one hell of a diversion. He'd have to come up with something spectacular. This was where Schmidt's model was going to be useful.

Carter slipped down the stairs as silently as he could. On the second floor he found the modem room. Nadya was standing in front of the modem, her hands held behind her head, the guard from downstairs, a huge brute of a man, holding his submachine gun on her and shouting for her to stretch out on the floor.

The guard pulled a walkie-talkie from his webbing. He

tried to operate it with one hand while holding the gun on her with the other.

Carter didn't wait to make a fancy play; he didn't have time. Hugo was in his hand and in the air in a split second. It caught the guard at the back of the neck and plunged through to the front. Blood poured from his burst carotid artery, covering Nadya's dark clothes from neck to crotch.

She screamed and fell to her knees, watching as the man slowly lowered himself to the ground.

"I'm sorry," she gasped, shivering and holding her arms across her chest. "I'm sorry I cried out. I was so frightened . . . and all the blood . . ."

"Don't talk about it," he said as he pulled his knife free and cleaned it on the guard's uniform. "Everything's okay now. Is the modem working?"

Her face looked paler, even under the black grease. "I got . . . your people . . . just a minute ago," she said, still unsteady. "The transmission wasn't the best. I've got the modem sending."

"How long will it take?"

"It's high speed. Twenty minutes. Maybe thirty."

"All right. I want you to go back to your apartment. Pack a bag, as little as you can. Put my stuff in as well. And wait for me there," he said, pulling her from the floor and holding her close. "All hell's going to break loose in a few hours. We've got to have a new hiding place."

She clung to him. "I don't want to go alone. I can't go alone," she said, her voice starting to show hysteria.

Carter held her at arm's length, and saw the wild fear in her eyes. Suddenly he struck her across the face, left then right. It wasn't his style, but he had to get her mind focused once again. He shook her until she stopped shivering and could look him at him, clear-eyed.

"I'll be all right," she said, shrugging free of his hands. "I'll go. I've got to get rid of all this blood."

"Tell me how to confirm with my people when this thing stops," he said.

"The red light will flash. If you want to talk, lift the receiver."

He knew she needed reassurance. He didn't want her to fold on him, or she'd be a handicap in the next phase. He reached for her and held her tight for a few seconds. "You did very well, Nadya. I'm very proud of you. But it's not over yet, okay?"

She reached up and pecked him on the mouth. "I'll be all right now. It was just so sudden," she said, her voice steady. "I'll go back home and be waiting for you."

When she was gone he checked his watch. He had at least ten minutes before the modem would be finished. He debated whether to get rid of the guard and, in the end decided there was just too much blood to clean up in the time he had.

He made a fast recon of the building, every floor and every corridor. Nadya had been wrong about their strength at night. He saw two more guards but managed to avoid them. When he got back to the modem the red light was flashing.

He picked up the receiver. "N3 here. You get it all?"

All he heard was the crackle of static on a bad line.

"N3 here. Did you get my signal?"

Still no answer.

"Shit! How the hell do I know if they got it or not?" he said aloud.

He ripped the tape reel from the modem, found a canister for it, sealed it with shipper's tape until it was waterproof, and slipped it inside his coveralls. The bulge looked like a fat pie plate sitting next to his gut.

When he left, it was by the front door. He slipped from the lighted area into shadows and found a small parking area to the right of the entrance. A battered little car, the

Russian version of the Italian Fiat, sat dejectedly by itself. He hot-wired the car, checked the gauges, and found he had enough gas for a tour of the town.

Carter pulled out without headlights and headed east beyond Katowice Prospekt to an area he hadn't seen before. Some old houses, a few partially demolished, were mixed with new. Few lights were on. A row of new houses sat across from a row of old, all deserted. One block further on, at the edge of habitation, sat another row of partially demolished old houses.

He returned to the science building, left the car where he'd found it, and entered the building again. It was quiet. He saw the two active guards still at work. Nothing appeared to be unusual.

Carter skirted the guarded area and let himself out the back door. In a couple of minutes he had sneaked past the couples and was on the sixth floor letting himself in Nadya's door.

She stood, shaking and wide-eyed in the middle of the room, the machine pistol pointed at him, her finger on the trigger. He took the pistol from her, clicked on the safety, and started to peel off his dark clothes.

She was all dressed and ready to go. The bloodstained coveralls and sweater were in the bathtub. "I want to change into some ordinary clothes," he said, taking her by the elbows and looking into her eyes. "Get the phone and wire we used to call my people. I've got to get them again."

While he dressed, she walked around like a zombie. When he was finished changing his clothes, he took the phone from her, opened the door, and made the connection at the terminal box quickly and quietly.

"Hawk? Carter."

"How's it going?"

"Touch and go here," Carter said. "But we'll make it. We sent a signal on the modem tonight, everything you could hope for, but I suspect they didn't pick it up."

"I talked to the captain of the *Ticonderoga* a half hour ago," the man in Washington said. "They were delayed. They talked to the woman, got your signal, but it was distorted."

"Damn! I've got the tape reel packed and ready to bring out. You're sure what they got is useless?"

"Not a hundred percent sure," Hawk admitted. Carter could picture him pacing up and down in his office, smoke pouring from the cheap cigar clamped between his teeth. "They'll try to decipher it all. They may get most of it, but it doesn't look good," he added. "What can we do at this end?"

"Keep the carrier on signal every midnight for the next three days. We may have a chance to send again."

"Good luck, Nick. We'll be looking for you on the Black Sea near the Bosporus," Hawk concluded.

Carter disconnected and rolled the loose wire around the phone.

Nadya was standing in the middle of the room, listening, her bag at her feet, her face chalky white. "I didn't think it would be like this," she said.

"It's always like this," he said, grinning. "What kind of spy school did you attend?"

He was enjoying himself now. He always did when he was in control. This was what his job was all about. It was all coming together now. He would pull off his plan at the Academy. He would take them out of here. They would all live happily ever after.

He hoped.

"What else do we have to do here?" she asked.

He looked around. She was taking too much. "Leave most of your clothes on hangers in the closet," he said, checking the small apartment. "They should find your personal things in the drawers."

He went in the bathroom and retrieved the bloody clothing. "We'll dispose of this but leave the bloodstains in the tub." He held the sweater out so some blood could drip on the floor.

"What is that all about?" she asked.

"And they told me you were a genius," he teased. "Let them think some unknown force took you and you're in bad shape. That way, when you're missing, you won't be a defector."

"That's brilliant! I was worried about my parents," she admitted.

A few minutes later they slipped out of the apartment, leaving the door unlocked.

TEN

Colonel Nikolai Ivanovich Gladkov sat at his desk, a dejected man. He wore his hat as usual. His riding crop sat on the massive desk in front of him. He curled one hand around it and began tapping it on the polished surface in time to the thoughts that kept pounding away inside his head.

Gladkov was a simple man. It was possible to gain a position of importance in the Soviet Union without being brilliant. Most truly brilliant people were slaves of the state. It took the politically oriented ones to make it to the top.

The colonel was politically oriented. Not necessarily to the politics of the party, but to the politics of organization. He knew what it took to please his superiors and he always went the extra mile to make sure he was seen in the right places at the right time doing what pleased his current commander.

His last posting had been in Poland. He'd been a major in charge of union-baiting in a manufacturing district. He had tricked more important Polish labor leaders into foolish acts of aggression than any other district commander. His

100

jails were always full. The agitation in his command had reached a low point.

It didn't matter that the lid was about to blow off in Poland when he was promoted and moved back to Moscow. That was his successor's problem. Anyone who had ever replaced Gladkov, on any job, had suffered reverses, but that never showed up in the wily colonel's record.

In Moscow he had been summoned to the Kremlin and a private interview with Morozov himself. The importance of Sukhumi had been explained. The rewards for keeping the vital scientific community free from danger were tangible. He could see himself in the uniform of a general and eventually marshal or even the director of the KGB, one of the most important men in the Soviet.

Everything had gone wrong from the start. The General Secretary had been foolish to move the Academy of Science in the first place, but Gladkov could never offer the opinion. He felt out of place with so many eggheads. It wasn't his style. He knew nothing about computers. The responsibility of guarding thousands of reels of tape the secrets of his government, the most recent developments in Soviet science—crowded in on him when he was alone. It scared the hell out of him.

The temper of labor unrest he could handle. Physical punishment came easy to him; it had always been his most reliable tool. But how did you deal with intellectuals? How did you protect something you didn't understand? The most simple theory of electrical forces was a total mystery to him. Computers were even beyond electrical theory in the hierarchy of his limited knowledge. Whether it was hardware, the machines that hummed in the building night and day, or the software that the scientists used to make it all work, the whole thing was like a strange puzzle to him.

But he had handled it well up to now. He refused to let anyone have an inkling of his lack of knowledge, insisting he knew how to handle the safety of the project without advice from the scientific community or his own people.

He, Gladkov, was in control and that's how it would be.

Except for the Spetsnaz, the special forces group. He couldn't stop them from sending the Spetsnaz, but he would control the bastards. No one had told him to relinquish one ounce of authority to anyone. So the Spetsnaz commander would damned well take orders from him.

His men had reported finding the dead guard in the modem room a half hour earlier. The colonel had ordered a thorough search of the Academy building and of every scientist's apartment. He didn't care that it was three in the morning. That was their problem.

One of the awakened physicists had ranted about the importance of finding the guard in the modem room. Something about the machines being the transmission stations for data. To hell with him. Let him rant and rave. Gladkov had cut off all communications out of Sukhumi. He couldn't shut down the electronic telephone exchange, but every access point was guarded. He would keep a lid on whatever the problem was until he was ready to report something that would be favorable to him.

"Sir?" His second in command knocked and entered.

"What is it, Major?" he asked, still whacking his baton on the desk in an even cadence.

"We have found the missing guard. He was stuffed in an old crate in the basement of the building. His weapon is missing."

A cold chill ran down Gladkov's spine. The spy Andropov had never been found. He had chosen to believe the man had left the territory and was content to let it go at that. But the bastard must have found a hiding place and was still at work.

"We found where the escaped prisoner has been hiding," the major added.

"What? Why the hell didn't you say so in the first place?" Gladkov screamed at him, his face flushed. "Where the hell was he?"

"One of the scientist's apartments, sir. We found a lot of blood in the bathtub and a trail of blood leading to the door."

"Who? What scientist?" he continued to rage, punctuating his questions with loud whacks of his crop on the shiny desktop.

"A woman, sir. Nadya Karpova."

"Has she been at work every day?" Gladkov asked.

"No one has been absent, sir."

"So he sneaked into her apartment in the last few hours, perhaps after he killed the guards. But how the hell could he do it?" Gladkov asked aloud as if talking to himself. "Madam Pivnev got off three shots. We could find only one bullet in the walls. Some blood was spilled that was not Pivnev's or his wife's."

He sat for a few minutes with his major standing at attention in front of the desk.

"There has to be more than one of them. Andropov broke out of jail, but he had to have accomplices. They had him stashed somewhere else. Or he's dead and the others are carrying on. There's no other explanation for it."

"We'll have to call Moscow, sir. Report the killings and the missing woman."

"We'll do no such thing, Comrade Major. Haven't you learned anything working with me?" he fumed, his face red. "We'll report this when we have more favorable information. And when the damned Spetsnaz arrive, you will have the commander report to me. The whole area is cut off from outgoing messages for everyone. Is that clear?" he said, standing to emphasize his point, his nose not five inches from the major's.

"Yes, sir."

"Who is this woman, Karpova?" Gladkov asked as he resumed his seat.

"Probably the most brilliant of them all, sir. She was a key member of their staff."

"Wouldn't you know. It couldn't be a minor clerk, could it. No matter. We keep the lid on. Nothing gets out of here until I order it. Is that clear?"

"No one. That includes all the scientific staff?" the major asked.

"No one. We shut down communications except for incoming traffic."

Gladkov suddenly thought of another detail that had escaped his attention. "How are they coming with the radar?" he asked. He had given the construction foreman an ultimatum: "Get the damned thing finished today or it's your head!"

"They finished the dish assembly at dusk today. Make that yesterday," the major said, looking at his watch.

"You'd better be right," the colonel growled. "I can't believe all the screw-ups you've permitted, Major. And it's all going down on your record."

"I'll get on—"

"What report do we have on the Spetsnaz?" Gladkov interrupted.

"They should be arriving at any time," the major said. "I've got a detail on the tarmac as a welcoming committee."

"I want to know the minute they check for their final approach," the colonel said. "Their leader, whoever he is, will be under my command from the first minute he lands. You got that?"

"Yes, sir."

"What have you set up for them?" Gladkov asked. "I told you to make it as primitive as possible. These men are trained to endure hardship, Major. We'll see that they get what they're trained for, right?"

"It's all arranged as you ordered, sir," the major reported, still at attention.

When the major had gone, Gladkov left the baton to roll on the tabletop and placed his hands on his knees. He let his massive swivel chair tilt backward until his hat pushed forward on his head. He closed his eyes. It was a position that was familiar to him. He would not create one wrinkle in his immaculate uniform while he got a few hours of sleep. He had an electric shaver in his desk that he would use in private when he awoke.

Let the bastards figure out how their commander never seemed to sleep. That was their problem. As he dozed off, a smile creased his normally stern countenance. Already he was beginning to enjoy what he would dish out to the Spetsnaz commander.

The little car remained where Carter had left it. No one was sniffing around the science building. Carter piled their few possessions, including a couple of blankets, into the back and took off as soon as Nadya was seated. She'd been quiet since they left the apartment, dogging his footsteps, keeping close to the shadows of the walls. The last couple of hours had been hard on her. She had killed a guard. They might never find out, but she knew. She knew she had killed one of her own and there was no going back.

Few vehicles were on the streets. Those that they saw drove fast with sirens screaming, heading for the Academy building. Someone had discovered their break-in. Carter wasn't surprised.

They passed Red Square and Katowice Prospekt before they were in total darkness except for their headlights. Carter pulled over and cut the lights.

"What are you doing? Let's get out of here!" Nadya hissed.

"I don't want to use the headlights. We need to build up our night vision," Carter said, putting an arm around her. She obviously was tired and still partially in shock, and she curled up in his arms, small and frightened. They sat with their own thoughts while waiting in the car, the darkness a cloak around them.

Slowly, as they watched, the eastern suburbs of the town started to unfold. At first they could only see the outlines of new houses, the walls solid but the roofs weird skeletons against the inky sky. As minutes passed they could see detail. The few trees that the construction people had not destroyed. The older houses spotted between the new. The piles of earth ready to be bulldozed around the raw foundations.

Finally, as their night vision improved, details stood out clearly. It was as if an infrared light had been shone on the scene, softly at first, then turned up by a giant rheostat until it gave them the gift of sight in a black void.

Carter took his arm from around Nadya and drove slowly, with all lights out, to the house he'd picked out earlier. One wall had been demolished. He drove the car into the room that had only three sides. He pulled a few scattered tree limbs, still green with leaves, across the opening. Inside, they selected a room with an old curtain across the cracked glass, spread the blankets, and lay curled in each others arms.

Carter heard Nadya breathing evenly within minutes. He was close to sleep but his mind was still working overtime. They had a long way to go before this one was over. The tape reel was uncomfortable. He pulled it from his shirt and put it on the floor beside him. They'd have to try one more transmit.

He curled into a ball under the thin blanket, shut off his mind, and fell asleep immediately.

The camouflaged Tupolov transport came in at dawn. Gladkov had a troop of his best regulars lined up on the tarmac to greet the new arrivals. While the twin jets screamed in reverse thrust as it passed less than fifty feet from the reception committee, the special forces warriors tumbled from the aircraft in a steady stream, found their footing, and lined up in front of the welcoming soldiers in parade order.

Gladkov, impressed by their spectacular dismount and swift formation, counted fifty men. Each was in camouflaged battle fatigues, complete with webbing that held a half-dozen grenades and a double-sided commando knife. Each man had a Kalashnikov at the ready, the model equipped for grenade launching.

They were an awe-inspiring group. They made Gladkov's reception committee look like parade-ground soldiers.

None of the men carried signs of rank or company designation. One man stepped from the end of the column. He marched to face Gladkov, saluted, and announced: "Colonel Dmitri Kondrati Rylev reporting."

Gladkov returned the salute casually. "You will accompany me in my car, Colonel. Arrangements have been made for your men."

"I will see to my men first, Colonel. I'll be at your office in a few minutes," the younger man said, turning on his heel and leaving Gladkov with his mouth open.

The Spetsnaz colonel was at least a head taller than Gladkov, and he must have weighed a good fifty pounds more than the KGB man. He was all muscle. Gladkov knew that the other colonel had learned a hundred ways to kill a man with his bare hands. He could kill with a comb, a ballpoint pen, a piece of writing paper.

It took his driver ten minutes to drive Gladkov to his office. He sat in his chair and waited, watching the hand of the clock on the opposite wall move, one minute at a time, until it changed from ten after six to twenty-nine past the hour.

Each minute he waited added to the fury of the Sukhumi KGB chief. This was his command. He had worked hard for it. And by God he was going to make that puppy toe the line.

David Hawk paced his office leaving a trail of foul smoke in his wake. Just as he was about to blow a fuse, his intercom rang. He punched the button savagely and yelled into the speaker.

"What is it?"

Ginger Bateman had put up with the old man for more years than she cared to count. She was used to his moods, understood the pressure he was under, and was usually calm in a sea of turmoil. "It's Howard."

Hawk punched the flashing button on his set. "What is it, Howard?" he growled.

"I've got some intelligence from one of our people in Moscow. General Secretary Morozov has ordered the Spetsnaz to prepare the whole damned collection of tapes for shipment home immediately. If Nick calls again, we should tell him that it might be too dangerous to go up against a special force of Spetsnaz. If he decides to go ahead with his plan, he's only got a day or two at the most."

"If he calls, I'll tell him about the time constraint. If I know our man, he won't change his plan," Hawk said, putting down the receiver and looking out his window but seeing nothing.

He slipped back into his chair and opened a folder. The whole thing was out of his hands now.

Rylev strode into Gladkov's office without saluting. He sat without being asked, poured himself a drink, and downed it before the startled Gladkov could react.

"What the hell do you think you are doing?" Gladkov sputtered, smashing his riding crop on the desk in front of the younger man.

Rylev snatched the crop from the colonel's hand and bent it easily until the dried leather inside snapped, leaving the shiny exterior leather the shape of a V, like a broken twig held together by bark alone.

"What I'm doing is taking over from an ineffective old fool," he said, leaning forward, a cruel grin on his face. "Our General Secretary is not a fool, Gladkov. He has spies everywhere. He knows this place is in great peril of destruction. So I am here. And I take command as of now."

"Never!" Gladkov shouted, looking at the broken crop with eyes that bugged out of his head. "Look what you've done." He shook his head, staring at the bent crop, then looked up at the Spetsnaz warrior with pure hatred in his eyes. "You are under my command and you will do what you are ordered. This base is sealed off at my order. That includes you. And you will deploy your men as I command."

"You stupid old man," Rylev said, pouring himself another vodka. "Do you think you can stand up to my men? Go ahead. Call Moscow. Either way you are finished here.

"Is the radar installation operative yet?" He shot the

question to the older man like the crack of a whip before Gladkov could respond.

"A few hours ago," a more subdued Gladkov answered.

"Have you questioned all the leading scientists? Do they have a clue what's going on here?"

"No," Gladkov said, still string at the broken crop.

"Tell me exactly what the situation is. I want every detail."

Gladkov's head dropped an inch or two as he began his recital. "A prisoner we were about to interrogate escaped. He broke into the home of the project chief. The intruder murdered the chief and his wife. He has entered the Academy building once that we know of, leaving two guards dead."

"One man?" Rylev asked, unbelieving. "One man did this in the midst of your garrison?"

"No. I'm sure it is a team of saboteurs," Gladkov said softly, his eyes moving from the broken crop to rest on his adversary. He was calmer, colder; his attitude was wait and see. He couldn't disguise his hatred for this man. After all, he was the hero of too many campaigns, in his own mind, to be subverted by this young upstart. His time would come. He would play it cagily in the meantime.

"Have you told me everything?" Rylev asked.

Gladkov came out of his musing, the question registering slowly as his mind raced to think about the last few days. "No," he said. "One other thing. One of our most brilliant scientists is missing, a woman. Her name is Nadya Karpova. I presume she's dead."

"And why do you presume? Do you have facts?"

"Her bath was covered in blood. A trail of blood led to her door. I'm sure she's dead."

"You old fool," Rylev said, dropping even the slightest show of respect for the older man. "If she was dead she would have been left in the tub. I know this woman. She has worked on many of our most secret projects," the young colonel went on, shaking his head at the stupidity of the older man. "I have to warn Moscow that someone is trying to take her out. Even now it might be too late."

ELEVEN

From a close-knit bower of low-hanging willow trees near a creek bed, Carter and Nadya Karpova lay on their bellies, looking through the branches at Spetsnaz troops deploying around town. Earlier they had seen a second aircraft deliver armored troop carriers to the special force.

Two Spetsnaz jogged by their position, their Kalashnikovs at the ready, the metal in their equipment creating a cadence to match their stride. They looked impressive, armed and deadly.

"Do you know how this changes your odds?" Nadya asked.

"I think so," Carter replied. "I estimate fifty or so of them."

"I mean the danger, not the numbers. I've made a study of the Spetsnaz. I was curious about them and had clearance to read their files," she said. "Did you know that each man carries three hundred rounds and fifty grenades for his AK-47? They have a bayonet that doubles as a saw and wire cutter, a P6 silenced pistol, and another knife that shoots a blade for more than thirty feet." She paused for a moment. "They're inhuman, Nick. I know from reliable

sources that they get their final training at their main training center, Zheltye Vody, in the Ukraine. It's near a group
of concentration camps. They use human subjects from the
camps to perfect their hand-to-hand killing techniques."

"What about a force like this one? What would it consist
of?" Carter asked. He didn't plan to go up against them by
himself, but plans could change and it was well to know
the enemy.

She thought about the question for a few seconds, recalling what she'd read. "A unit like this will have a senior
and a junior officer, a communications man, a medic, at
least two demolitions experts, and four reconnaissance experts," she said. "The communications men have 'burst'
communications transmitters that send a short 'squirt' of
encoded messages back to headquarters by satellite to be
encoded."

Carter listened intently. His plan would be shot to hell if
they had demolitions experts who could defuse a nuclear
device; they'd spot Schmidt's model for what it was. He'd
have to take out the town's communications and the 'burst'
transmitters as well. This was getting too damned compli-
cated, he thought. "Do they carry special insignia?" he
asked.

"Which ones?" she asked.

"The demolitions experts and the communications men.
Can I pick them out if I have to?"

"I don't believe they have insignias. But the demolitions
men guard their equipment jealously. It's a small four-
wheel-drive truck with a bombproof trailer attached. They
practically live out of it. The 'burst' transmitters never
leave the sight of the communications men. They are
painted red and are carried on special webbing on their
backs."

While he was thinking he'd have to eliminate the demolitions men, and the special transmitters, she was going on with her lecture.

"They are the best of the best," she explained. "They are picked for their fearlessness and cruelty . . . like a horde of robots." She shuddered.

Carter stared hard at her serious, beautiful face. "Are you having second thoughts about what we're doing?" he asked.

"No, not at all. It's just that it will be such an irreversible change. My homeland . . . everyone I know . . . I'll be leaving it all—forever."

"I'm not worried about you changing your mind. The decision has been fermenting in that head of yours for too long."

"That's very true," she said, nodding slowly. "But I can't quite believe where we are and what we're doing. And we have so much to do yet. The odds are all against us," she went on, a strange wonder in her eyes, "and yet you seem so calm. You infect me with it. I really believe you'll pull it off, even with these brutes parading around town."

"Just continue to believe," he said. "We're going to destroy the tapes and we'll use one of your plans."

"One of my plans? I don't remember . . ."

"You may have been kidding around, but you gave me a hell of an idea. And it's going to be beautiful, a great plan. You'll recognize the idea when you see it in action," he said with a chuckle as he poked his face out of the greenery to get the lay of the land.

"Please, Nick! You've got to tell me!"

"Sssh. We can make it back to the house now," he said, taking her hand and guiding her between the trees to the next block and the old house where they had been holed up.

* * *

Taking advantage of the late-afternoon shadows, Carter moved around town unseen. He sprinted between buildings, keeping to the alleys, moving from one end of town to the other, making sure he knew every street and every building.

One new structure, almost a miniature of the Academy building, was not guarded. No lights were showing.

Carter slipped the lock. He moved cautiously, relying on his night vision, examining every room with care. It was another scientific building. Some of the computer equipment looked like the stuff he'd seen in the modem room.

He picked up a phone beside one of the machines. A dial tone hummed in his ear. The system was modern electronic. Nadya had explained they could dial anywhere in the world if you knew the right codes. She was one of the few with the right codes.

He returned to the door, peeked out cautiously, and snaked out on silent feet into the night, heading for the old house and Nadya.

The decrepit house where she waited was one of three. Theirs was the only one partly demolished. As he drew closer, he thought he saw a shadow close to a back window.

He crept toward the shadow, careful not to snap any of the small dry twigs that had fallen from the trees. A Spetsnaz warrior was looking in a back window. He had just taken his special projectile knife from its case and was priming it to fire its missile. Nadya had told him it was capable of sending a blade thirty feet. Carter had no time to waste. He slipped Hugo into his palm and let fly.

The stiletto was off target, piercing the man's arm just above the elbow. The Russian soldier dropped his special weapon but turned in Carter's direction, slipped the safety off his AK-47, and braced himself for a fight.

The black shadow that was the Killmaster came on as

fast as his legs would carry him. He took the special forces man at the knees and bowled him over. In the struggle for supremacy, Carter snatched the stiletto from the man's arm and plunged it up through his ribs.

The Kalashnikov slid in the grass out of sight. Carter was sure the knife had sliced into the heart, but the man fought on. The Russian, a young, strong, blond giant, went for his all-purpose knife and brought it around as Carter's free hand caught it.

The Soviet soldier was incredibly strong. They rolled in the grass, Carter holding the knife hand, his other free with the deadly Hugo looking for an opening.

A grenade popped loose from the man's webbing. The release caught on a tree root and primed the deadly weapon.

Blood streamed from the man's mouth. His strength was ebbing and his eyes glazed as they fought. Carter couldn't find another opening for his knife, but it wasn't needed. Somehow the man had fought on with one chamber of his heart pumping blood into his chest cavity.

Five or six seconds had passed since the grenade had been armed. Carter rolled the dying man on top of the tree root and darted away. The explosion lifted the body two feet from the ground. The soft flesh caught all the grenade fragments like a catcher's mitt while Carter lay prone a few feet from the concussion.

The Killmaster pulled himself from the damp ground and raced for the house. Nadya was waiting for him. She had seen the struggle. "Where's the reel of tape?" he called to her as he came in the front door.

"Here," she said, handing it to him.

"Come on! We don't have much time!" he rasped. "Got to get the hell out of here!"

She was dressed in dark blue pants and a navy sweater. She tied a dark scarf around her hair and followed him out the door, not bothering with any of their few possessions.

"We're going to leave him there?" she asked.

"The shit's hit the fan, as we say back home. We don't have time to bury him," he said over his shoulder as he dragged her through darkened streets to the building he'd found. "I came across this place tonight," he said when they were in the darkness of the smaller building. "It looks like they have modems here and the phones have a dial tone. Why didn't you tell me about this place?"

"I've never been here," she said. "Show me the modems."

"They're not wireless. We can't send to the *Ticonderoga*," she said, examining the modems and putting the tape reel in one. "Got a special number we can call?"

He dialed in AXE's computer and coded in his own special recognition signals.

"Hello, N3," the honeyed voice of the computer answered.

"Can you connect me to a modem immediately?" he asked.

"Of course."

"Do it. When the transmission is finished, tell Hawk you've got it," he said.

Nadya waited for the signal and started the transmission on its way. They waited in silence for the tape to end.

"We'll have to sleep in the hills tonight," Carter said at last. But Nadya was deep in thought and didn't seem to hear him.

"Am I going to see you when you get back there, to America?" she asked, her voice sounding like a small girl's, a pleading voice, a voice asking if there really was a Santa Claus.

"As often as we can," he said truthfully, knowing and regretting that it would be seldom. "As often as we can."

TWELVE

The *Ticonderoga* was anchored in the lea of the Greek island of Limos less than a hundred and fifty miles from Istanbul. Two men sat in the chart room drinking coffee and smoking cheroots. The small, strong cigars were a weakness of Captain Martin Jameson, but he shared them with his officers.

Commander Gerry Orwell sat in the chart room with Jameson. They were alone, casually taking stock of the action. It had been a long day and an eventful one compared to the journey that had brought them from the Atlantic Ocean task force. None of the ships on patrol along the Israeli and Lebanese coasts could be spared. The Hormuz situation was well in hand. They'd been the ones who'd dropped Carter off, so they were it. To Jameson, who had not minded making the drop, it now seemed like sending a whole navy to destroy a fishing trawler. But he didn't have all the details. Obviously someone thought what Carter was sending out was important.

"We're supposed to wait for a communication, then send a squadron of multimillion-dollar choppers into the

Bosporus to pick up this spook?" Jameson asked.

"They said to send a whole fucking squadron if the spook wanted it," Orwell said. "The guy has clout like you wouldn't believe. You've got to admire the bastard," he went on. "We're surrounded by steel and firepower. He's got only his wits between him and the Russians. That's it." He shook his head.

"I'm not sure of our orders from here on in," Orwell went on. "I've got to get the choppers in the air soon, but what comes after?"

"The original plan. Standing by for transmissions by modem," Jameson said, putting his feet on the metal chart table. He was weary. He'd get a couple of hours of shut-eye soon. "When the spook has done his job he's going to try to get himself and a Soviet woman out by way of the Black Sea. We're to patrol the waters five to ten miles beyond the Bosporus."

"I don't envy the poor bastard his escape plan," Orwell said. "Why didn't he just order up our chopper again to take him out?"

"Sorry. Forgot to tell you when you were busy contacting our people back home," Jameson said, taking his feet from the table and standing, heading for the door. "I've had a signal that the Russians have almost activated their new radar. The spook's sure they'll have it in service before he makes his break."

"Bad luck."

"Tells you something about the guy, doesn't it," Jameson said as he opened the chart room bulkhead door. "He's not willing to risk our chopper when their radar's up and working. Sounds like he's a right guy."

Orwell sat alone thinking about the town of Sukhumi and what it would be like to be behind enemy likes living on your wits. He looked around at the thick steel bulkhead and thought about the squadrons of fighters in the belly of the ship.

No way he would trade. No way.

"My men are deployed at strategic locations," Colonel Rylev said as he barged into Gladkov's office. "There is no way the Americans are going to penetrate."

Gladkov had undergone a change since their last meeting. He had tested his will against the younger man and found himself lacking. He'd been around too long. Not as long as the graybeards at headquarters, but for a man still in charge of front-line troops he had let progress pass him by. He didn't know all the new weaponry or the hand-to-hand techniques he ought to know. He had let himself get soft. Too many years of living a lie, a con man with the eternal bluff always ready to trot out nice and shiny, he had finally begun to wind down. He was tired. He was tired of the façade, the hat always in place, the mystique he created and wore like a false face, a veneer to hide the dry rot underneath. He felt as if he'd just looked in the magic mirror and been told he wasn't the fairest of them all. It was deflating. He felt old and weary.

"How many do you think there are?"

"Hard to tell. More than one from what I've seen. My men will make short work of them," Rylev said. He was an excellent judge of men and of reading their motivations. His skills with people as well as with the rigors of the training were what had taken him so far so soon. He recognized Gladkov's surrender and understood it better than the older man would have guessed. And he was charitable for a man who dealt in violent death. He won battles in more ways than one and he saw no sense in pulverizing a man when he was down. If it was all a bluff, then that was another matter. If the scenario changed, he would cut the KGB man down to size.

"Have you been in touch with your people in Moscow?" Gladkov asked.

"Just a minor update. They are satisfied."

"What do you think the Americans are after?" Gladkov asked.

"The storage of scientific data. To destroy it somehow. They must think we are idiots if they think they can get to it."

"We were idiots for putting it here in the first place."

"Be careful of your tongue, Nikolai Ivanovich Gladkov. The General Secretary himself ordered the Academy of Science moved here."

"Did you know this was his hometown?" Gladkov asked.

"What difference does that make?" Rylev replied.

"A political move," Gladkov said, always the political animal. "A test of strength. He sends vital information to his hometown, creates massive activity, employment, prosperity, then moves the Academy back to Moscow."

"I repeat: What difference does that make?" Rylev asked. "I do my job and you do yours. If you ask too many questions, you spend the rest of your life in a very cold climate."

"Just so, Dmitri Kondrati Rylev. The General Secretary can play his games, but if we fail to protect his ass, the Americans will destroy all that has been built for the last ten years or more. Will he go to the gulags? I doubt it."

"This is very dangerous talk, Colonel," Rylev said, beginning to get angry.

"Forget it. Forget I ever spoke. But remember this," Gladkov added. "You asked for command here. You wanted it and you can have it. But you'd better not fail or we're all in deep trouble. Very deep trouble."

* * *

Carter felt better about the mission when they sneaked out of the building and headed for the hills. This time he was sure the modem transmission had gone through.

"Where are we going?" Nadya asked.

"I have some hidden supplies," he said. "How are you at hiking?"

"I can keep up with you," she told him.

Carter took the lead, pushing his way through low scrub, avoiding treacherous crevices, walking around huge boulders that blocked their way. He never lost his concentration, always aware of what lay ahead and on each side. It took them fifteen minutes of climbing at a steady rate to reach a spot close to the hiding place for his ATV. Nadya caught up, breathing hard.

"What is it?" she asked.

"Quiet! Someone's been here," he said, pointing to the broken bushes in front of them. "Get down behind that boulder. I want to take a look around."

He made his way through the brush to a spot overlooking the crevice where he'd hidden the vehicle. The camouflage cover had been pulled aside and the ATV was gone.

The chatter of an automatic rifle split the night air. The ground around him was churned up by 7.62mm slugs, one taking the leather from the toe of his boot.

Wilhelmina was in his hand. There was no need for a silent kill now. He hoped the sound of gunfire wouldn't reach town. It was only three miles and it was a quiet night.

A blast of gunfire shattered the rock in front of him. He caught the muzzle flash and bracketed it with two shots. Another Kalashnikov started up to his left. Chips of rock stung his cheek and blood ran to his chin. Hi fired blindly, instinctively, and the Russian weapon continued to fire in a steady stream, sending small missiles of death skyward until a cold finger tensed on an empty clip.

Carter waited a few seconds and crept to the position of the first attacker. He found the man, an army regular, wounded but not dead. A 9mm slug had torn at his neck. He was bleeding to death.

He concentrated on the second man. By the time he got to him, Nadya was standing over the body, her submachine gun pointed at his head.

"What's happened?" she whispered. "They found your cache, didn't they."

Carter nodded. "They've found the vehicle."

"Are we without supplies?" she asked. She was shaking again. "Do we have to go back?"

He shaded his eyes from the ball of fire that was settling toward the horizon off to their left. It was after six. "See that hill off to the right, maybe seven miles?" he asked, pointing.

"Yes. It's got something on it."

"Radar. It wasn't there the last time I was here. My main camp is on the other side of that hill."

"Do you think they found it?"

"I didn't think they'd find this. There's no way of knowing without taking a look."

"Go ahead. I'll follow. We've got to know."

He headed out at a steady pace, They'd have to take a roundabout route. They'd be lucky if they made four miles an hour in this terrain, even at a breakneck pace. He sure as hell didn't want to be scouting the hill after dark.

Stewart Freeman's office at State was on the fifth floor. It was plush, as befitted a man who had been in the intelligence community for twenty years then joined State where he'd nursed a constant succession of men who had been appointed to run the State Department. David Hawk had been in the office for only a few minutes. He sat, almost lost in a huge wing chair, one of his cheap cigars creating a toxic cloud around him.

Freeman sat behind a huge oak desk in an executive swivel chair, the type of chair that was only assigned to the highest level of staff in the government hierarchy. The chair was a triumph of one-upmanship in the daily battle of running the country. The small, bald man, his appearance in direct contrast to his influence, was holding a tape reel canister in his hand, a broad smile on his face.

"I owe you one for this, David, old friend," he said. "Do you have any idea what's on this thing?"

"My man is usually very thorough," Hawk said, smiling to himself. "I'm sure it contains a number of interesting goodies." He'd made a copy of it before handing it over to State and was having some of AXE's experts review its contents. He hadn't yet seen the report.

"Whoever put it together orchestrated a masterpiece," Freeman said. "Their 'star wars' research is advanced well beyond ours. We've got it all here," he crowed, waving the canister at Hawk. "Their newest fighter, a Foxstar, one advanced beyond their Foxbat and Foxhound series. It's beautiful. Their latest missile cruiser, their work on artificial intelligence, the advances they've made with robotry and the electronics wizardry they've stolen from the Japanese. It's all here and much more."

"I'm glad that you're pleased," Hawk said as a secretary came in with coffee and Danish.

"We have to destroy the whole storage area, David," Freeman said. "This reel is a coup beyond the scope of anything the CIA has done in years, but imagine the effect of destroying their whole repository."

"It would set them back for years," Hawk mused.

Freeman leaned forward to make his point. He had crumbs from a cruller on his mustache. "It's more than that," he said, his eyes glowing. "Morozov made the biggest mistake any General Secretary of the Soviet Union ever made when he moved the data to Sukhumi. He would be discredited. The Politburo would be in a turmoil. Infighting would go on for years. They could no longer form a united front against the free world. They wouldn't have the scientific data to use as a sword over our heads," the small man went on. "It's so big, your man *has* to make it work."

"He'll make it work, Stewart," Hawk said calmly. "Nick will make it work."

The new cave they'd found was a couple of miles south of the fissure where Carter had hidden the ATV. They had found the cache of supplies intact, slept through the night and part of the morning, and picked out what they could strap to their backs.

Nadya had the naturally curious mind of the gifted scientist. The model of the atomic bomb fascinated her.

"Let me do it," she pleaded like a child. "I'm good at this kind of thing, you'll see."

He hadn't been looking forward to doing the assembly himself. He was a man of action and had a lot of ground to cover before they could use the bomb. "It's all yours. I've got something else to do."

"What is it, Nick? Do you need me?"

"I've got to check out the Spetsnaz communications and their bomb squad. And somehow I've got to destroy the whole Sukhumi communications setup."

She stood and came to him. "I'm afraid for you," she said as she clung to him.

"Don't worry. It's what I do best. If they have communications and demolitions men, our plan can't work."

He held her at arm's length. The light from the small propane lamp cast gigantic shadows against the wall of the cave. He kissed her softly on the lips and eased her down beside the lamp.

"Have the bomb finished when I get back," he said, pulling on the dark outfit again, "and be ready to move."

"How long will you be?" she asked

"A couple of hours. Maybe three. Remember, be ready when I get back. We've got to get the bomb in the computer building," he said as he pulled the camouflage cover from the cave entrance. "It's going to be a long night."

THIRTEEN

The Spetsnaz camp was primitive but efficiently set up. The only fault Carter could find with it was the way specialists stuck together. Small groups sat together around their fires, their tents pitched nearby. Carter estimated that half of them were on patrol or guarding the science building.

He made a soft probe of the perimeter. Guards were set out at regular intervals. The Killmaster had to infiltrate, zero in on his targets, kill them, dispose of their bodies, and get the hell out.

By the time he had circled the perimeter, Carter had formulated his plan. He would hit the two communications men first; they looked like the easiest. He decided that the demolitions men seemed to be the toughest targets; he would need a Spetsnaz uniform to get close to them. The ones with the transmitters were holed up in a cave by themselves. The Killmaster knew they had made a bad choice.

Carter crawled past the outposts, skirting the sentries by only a few feet. At the mouth of the cave, he stopped, peeled Pierre from his inner thigh, and held the small bomb

127

in his right hand. He crawled to the mouth of the cave, turned the two halves of the bomb, held his breath, and tossed the bomb between the two Spetsnaz.

They looked up, surprised, and then down at their feet where the two halves of the bomb were still spinning on the flat rock. One grabbed at his throat and crumpled to the ground. The other still had breath in his lungs. He started to go for his gun but was unable to hold his breath long enough to complete the maneuver. The P6 pistol dropped from his fingers and clattered down the rock leading from the cave.

A hand curled around the side of the cave and scooped up the gun. Carter waited. No one below in the camp made a move toward the cave.

He waited a minute before he went in. The relative openness of the cave had carried the gas away but not before it had done its job.

Out of sight of the camp he stripped the two bodies, then dumped them at the back of the cave. He destroyed their communicators, the red cylinders Nadya had described.

One of the uniforms was a perfect fit, the other small enough for Nadya to use. The Spetsnaz men were picked for size and strength. This one must have been one hell of a radioman, Carter thought. With difficulty, he put on both uniforms, one over the other.

It was time to move out again. The easiest way to get from point A to point B was to stop and talk with each group as they passed, accept cigarettes, and take a swig of vodka.

It seemed that the Spetsnaz were not very different from their army brothers worldwide. Bottles of the fiery liquid were everywhere. Obviously the General Secretary's edict of forced sobriety wasn't working here.

The demolitions men were off to themselves at the perimeter of the camp. Sentries walked their posts not twenty yards from them. Others sat at their campfires.

Carter knew he would have to hide their bodies in their own demolition chamber. Somehow he had to get to them separately, disable them, and stuff them in their trailer.

He joined them for a smoke. One was a man about his size, the other a few pounds heavier. "Another boring assignment, comrades," he said.

"As usual," the larger of the two said. He was sitting on Carter's right. The other was across the fire. All three were out of sight of the rest of the camp.

This was a tricky situation, he knew. These two were skilled killers. They were demolitions experts, but first and foremost they were killers. It didn't help that a score of Spetsnaz like them sat at campfires within earshot or that someone could find the dead men in the cave at any moment.

It would have to be quick and it would have to be silent. When he went for one, the other would react like a coiled spring

He pulled a cigarette from a crushed pack in his borrowed tunic. The blazing embers that flared in front of him were all too big to use as a lighter. "Got a light?" he asked the man beside him.

As the big man leaned close, cupping a match in his hands, the flames partly hid him from his partner. The Killmaster grasped his tunic with his right hand and slipped Hugo between his ribs in one fluid motion. While the man died, he was held erect for a second or two as Carter readied himself for an attack.

He couldn't let him slip into the fire. Any outroar from his partner would be heard. The whole thing had to seem normal.

"What's the matter with him?" Carter asked, still holding the man erect, bunching his tunic in his left fist, the stiletto behind the man's back. "Is he sick or what?"

"What the hell you talking about? He's never sick . . ." the demolitions man said as he scrambled around the campfire. This was his camp. He had been sitting with his partner. Everyone here was Spetsnaz.

He was halfway through the sentence and leaning over his friend when the blade found his heart. It was a killing thrust. Like his friend, not a word was formed by his lips as the blood drained from his heart to flood his upper torso before the muscle stopped pumping.

It had all been so easy up to now. Four of the deadliest fighters alive had given up their lives without a sound. Carter knew it wouldn't all be this easy. His next move was to pile them in the demolition chamber and pull it out of there.

Carter dumped the bodies in the chamber, a steel-reinforced box on a trailer usually pulled by a four-wheel-drive vehicle. The box was used to detonate bombs the team couldn't defuse.

"What's going on here?" A sergeant appeared out of the gloom as the bodies disappeared.

Carter froze in the act of closing the lid.

"You know how it is, Sergeant," the Killmaster said as a cold sweat broke out beneath his uniforms. "The colonel wants to show off our equipment to the local guy. That other colonel, the one with the hat."

"At night?" the sergeant asked suspiciously. "Nobody told me."

"So what else is new, comrade? They tell you everything?" Carter asked, regaining his cool.

"Sounds like you guys got yours at last," the sergeant said with a laugh. "You smart-ass demolition bastards got it easy. Where's your partner?"

"Taking a leak. Be back in a minute."

"Maybe a little extra duty's just what you need," the

sergeant said as he moved off to another campfire.

Carter sauntered to the truck and backed it up. He had to get out and couple the trailer to the hitch with a dozen pairs of eyes on him. Finally he drove off through the sentry lines and around to the other side of the camp.

He left the truck behind a rocky outcropping where a few moonbeams sneaking through the cloud cover bathed the scene in light. No one would find it unless they were looking for it.

He was taking the whole operation one step at a time and with great care. For the Killmaster, his assignment was to destroy the science building and the tapes. He couldn't do that if he was dead.

Carter was walking up Nesterov Boulevard on the west side of Red Square when the men were found in the cave. He was too far away to hear the commotion the discovery created. He rounded the corner leading to Novaza Prospekt and saw the row of big old houses he'd seen before and catalogued in his mind. He could pick out KGB headquarters. The communications building was located at the rear of the KGB building. He threaded his way through patrols of Spetsnaz troops and a few regulars hanging around their own headquarters.

"Got a light?" a Spetsnaz soldier asked. He was standing behind a tree, guarding one of the big houses.

Carter reached for his lighter with one hand and snaked the Spetsnaz double-sided knife from its scabbard with the other.

While the enemy soldier took the light, Carter looked up and down the street. This one was too close to the action to leave as he was. No one was looking their way. He drove the knife up through the other man's diaphragm and shoved with all his strength, turning the blade, carving up the chambers of the Russian's heart. This was turning out to be a killing ground and it would get worse. He preferred sub-terfuge to outright killing, but he could play it either way.

He sat the body against the bole of the tree out of sight and wiped his knife on his camouflage pants. He walked slowly toward the KGB house and strolled past more troops unchallenged until he made it to the communications shack. He stopped in the shadows of the building and took two primed packages of C4 from his pack. With them in one arm and the AK-47 in the other, he kicked down the door and went in shooting.

Three men sat at a long table, hundreds of switches and a dozen consoles in front of them. They looked around in surprise and reached for hand weapons as Carter opened up. The 7.62mm slugs lifted them from their chairs and flung them against the monitors.

Carter set the timers on the two charges at ten seconds and positioned them against the incoming cables and the leads to discs on the roof. He ran from the shack yelling at the top of his lungs. "They're in the communications room! Get the bastards!"

Every soldier in sight rushed to the small building. Some made it inside. Others made it to the door only to be blown to fragments as the full force of the C4 blew.

Carter was curled behind a tree. Only one man nearby had survived. He was smaller than most of his fellows. He was looking at the American with hatred in his eyes, un-slinging his rifle.

Carter got him in the throat with the projectile knife. The man looked surprised. The blade was stuck in his neck. Blood poured down his uniform. He tried to reach for the blade as his eyes began to glaze and his knees buckled. The man from AXE ran to him quickly, pulled off his boots and hat, then disappeared in the maze of new houses leading to the hills outside of town.

* * *

The cave was transformed. The propane lamp was turned down to a dull glow. Psychedelic lights played on the walls and ceiling of the irregular rock. Where the rock was damp with seepage, the colors were more vivid.

In the center of the cave a live thing sat. It was the size of a household water tank—a shining silver cylinder with rows of lights running along two paths on its top. The lights were red and orange, flicking on and off, tracing a pattern back and forth across its surface. In the middle of the cylinder, a square box had been attached. A liquid crystal display was ticking off a countdown in large red numerals amid a battery of buttons. The object looked very real. It produced the effect desired on the Killmaster as he stood and looked at it, his mouth slightly open.

"That's unbelievable," he said after a long interval. Even knowing that it was a fake, it produced a degree of awe.

"It won't look as scary in better light," she said, obviously proud of her work.

"I didn't realize it came with batteries. Will they last long enough?"

She reached for the bomb and pressed a hidden switch on the side of the countdown clock. The lights went out and the cave was transformed from a fairyland to a hole in the rock.

"We should try to cut the power in the new building. I'll have to give it some thought," he said as she turned up the propane lamp.

"I heard the explosions," Nadya said. "Did your plans work?"

"Well enough."

"Did you have to kill many men?"

He knew that she was going through a difficult time. These were her people. He decided to play it down.

"I did what was needed. I don't like killing."

She came to him and put her arms around him. "I know," she said. "It's not easy for either of us."

They were speaking English. She had insisted she be allowed the practice every time they were alone. "What happens next?" she asked, obviously eager to get on with the job and be on her way out of Sukhumi.

"I managed to get two Spetsnaz uniforms." He stepped back and started peeling off the outer one. "And from now on we must speak only Russian."

This was the critical time. It would work or it would blow from this point on and they had to be on their toes every minute. "We take your science project to the computer center and set it up," he said. "We warn officialdom that it is an American bomb, then we let them stew over it while we come back here and change into our Soviet uniforms."

"What if they try to work on the bomb while we are back here?"

"They won't. Before we go we'll make sure they know it's booby-trapped," she said. "One problem is the weight. It should be too heavy to move, and basically it's a fancy tin can."

"That's not a problem," she said, smiling in the dim light. He had stripped off the smaller uniform by this time and she was down to her underwear. "One end of the bomb isn't glued," she explained. "We fill it with blank computer tapes and glue the end back. The bottom of the cylinder is metal. I know where they keep some powerful magnets in a special storeroom away from the computer tapes. We can leave the bomb on a section of metal floor with magnets between the floor and the bomb. It would take a circus strongman to budge it."

Carter grinned. "You really are a genius. There's no reason why that wouldn't work." When they were both dressed in their Spetsnaz uniforms, he gave her a brief hug.

"Let's go, smart lady," he said, releasing her and wrapping the bomb in the camouflage cloth from the cave entrance and carefully hoisting it over one shoulder. "Let's get this show on the road."

FOURTEEN

The fake bomb was relatively light. Slung in the camouflage cloth, it stuck out at both ends, but Nadya covered those ends with pieces of a backpack. Carter started down the hill from their camp with Nadya at his heels. Halfway down they switched, Nadya taking the load while Carter took the lead.

They passed two- and three-man patrols of Spetsnaz and occasionally a troop carrier shuttling the men around. The army regulars assigned to the KGB didn't seem to be in evidence.

They neared the Academy building.

"How are you going to play it?" Nadya asked.

"We're going into one of the apartment buildings and coming out the back to the center court," Carter told her, whispering over his shoulder as they covered the ground quickly. "You remember the first time? It's surrounded by the apartments, but the Academy building opens up at one end. We go in the back door again. I figure they'll have fewer guards out back."

Just as he finished, an explosion shook the whole town.

136

Carter wasn't sure what it was, probably a residue of his attack on the communications building.

Nadya followed Carter into the front entrance of the apartment building and out the back. They kept moving, passing everyone they met without being challenged. She had cut her hair short. The uniform was a little too large but not noticeable.

The buildings were abnormally quiet. The Academy building had been evacuated and the scientists obviously ordered to stay indoors. They would be curious, looking out the windows, but after the explosion they would be looking out the front. The few who looked out the back would see two Spetsnaz, one carrying a heavy load and that wasn't too unusual.

Two Spetsnaz guards were at the back door, their automatic weapons slung over their shoulders. They were obviously confused by the explosion.

"Where the hell do you think you're going?" one said, unslinging his rifle.

"Orders from the colonel. This piece of equipment has to go inside," Nadya said in as deep a voice as she could muster. She muscled her way past the guards.

"What is it?" the guard asked.

"You think I'm an egghead scientist?" Nadya shot back continuing to walk. "How the hell should I know?"

"Halt!" one of them shouted.

Carter had his Luger in his hand. He slipped it out of sight behind his back. His stolen AK-47 was slung over the other shoulder, the safety off, a round jacked into the chamber.

"I told you to halt!" the guard shouted again.

The other guard had his rifle at the ready now. He pulled back the cocking lever as Carter shot him through the head.

The second guard stood rigid, dumbfounded at seeing his partner go down at the hands of one of their own men.

His finger tightened on the trigger. Carter put two slugs through his heart.

"What do we do now?" Nadya said, her face pale. This was for real. She was facing death too often. Two dead men lay at the back door as they moved on to the center of the building.

"Keep going. We're going to plant this dead center in the building," Carter ordered. "If anyone challenges us now, we eliminate them."

Carter led the way through the maze of aisles to the middle of the first floor. He helped Nadya unsling her burden and uncover it. They centered it on the metal floor. She went for the magnets. When they were attached, they held it firm.

"I don't think we need to fill it," she said, glueing the end as she spoke. The whole operation took no more than five minutes.

"Looks real," Nadya admitted.

"You did a great job," Carter said, turning on the switch that activated the internal batteries. Rows of small amber and red lights started to run in a pattern across the top of the cylinder. A liquid crystal display showed sixteen hours and counting.

They could hear feet pounding their way. Two Spetsnaz wheeled around the corner and took two slugs each from Carter's Luger.

"God! More killing!" Nadya cried. "When will it ever end?"

Carter didn't have time to answer. Two regular army soldiers came skidding around the far end of the aisle and Nadya picked them off with the 9mm P6 Carter had taken with the uniform. It had been an automatic reaction. Even in the act of mourning her own people, she did what she had to do.

"All hell's going to break loose soon," Carter said.

"Let's shut down the electricity and get out of here!"

Electric power entered the building through a cable in the basement. They ran along lighted aisles to the stairs and were in the basement in seconds. No one was there. Carter told her to stay back while he pulled the pins on two grenades. He held the clips in his palms, keeping them from firing until he had placed them on either side of the cable. He let them go and dived behind the partition wall where Nadya waited.

They clung to each other as the whole basement shook. They didn't have to check on the result: total darkness enveloped them.

"Hang on to my belt," he shouted as the noise reverberated in the cement-walled basement. He took off as fast as he could along the route he had memorized. They ran past the bomb on the first floor and toward the front entrance.

As they emerged into the night, covered from head to foot in cement chips and plaster dust, they were met by a Spetsnaz officer and a half-dozen men climbing out of a troop carrier.

"Don't go in there!" Carter gasped, acting scared and out of breath. "A nuclear device is set to blow. The American spies have planted a bomb in there!"

"Did you see it?" the officer asked incredulously.

"Yes," Carter said, nodding rapidly. "Ugly machine, a timer on top. I think it's booby-trapped. We need the demolitions men, sir."

It was the first time Colonel Rylev had seen men under his command lying dead, their blood spilled on Soviet soil, since he took his training with the Spetsnaz ten years earlier.

Two men were sprawled near the strange object, their eyes staring at the ceiling, dull and lifeless, their chests punctured with 9mm slugs from guns of his own force.

Two others were draped over computer frames nearby, their backs torn by exit holes, rib bones shining white in contrast to the blood spread through the scene.

"Take the bodies away from that damned thing," he ordered two soldiers standing by, their faces reflecting the hatred and dread that he felt.

As he looked at it in horror, the silver object, partly covered with blood, blinked red and orange as strings of small lights left no doubt that, whatever it was, it had a life of its own.

"Get me the demolitions men," he ordered, his voice low, lacking the usual crisp air of command.

"They're missing, sir," one of the men said. "Don't you remember . . . ?"

"Yes, yes. I remember," he snapped, recalling the discovery of the dead men in their own demolition chamber.

While he was trying to decide what to do next, Colonel Gladkov strode into the middle of the Academy building followed by two of his junior officers. "What's this?" he asked.

"I don't know, Colonel," he said. "I've lost at least four more men. This thing looks dangerous. We'd better leave it alone until we know what it is."

The reply didn't carry the same condescending tone the Spetsnaz colonel had used in the past few hours. He had lost his demolitions men and his communications experts, Gladkov's communications had been destroyed and now this, whatever it was. He had been defeated on his own battleground by enemies he was yet to see. Already he was trying to decide what he was going to tell Moscow.

"I know what it is," one of Gladkov's officers said, backing away involuntarily.

"Well, tell us, comrade. Speak up!" Gladkov said, his voice more authoritative now that Rylev had proved fallible. He beat on his uniform trousers with a new riding crop, impatient for the answer.

"I took a special course in American nuclear devices. That's what this is. A portable nuclear device, about half a megaton, but it's enough to destroy this town and anything else within a mile and a half."

"Well, don't just stand there, comrade. Get busy and defuse it!" Gladkov ordered.

"I don't know how. My course was for recognition only. The damned thing has a timer. It looks like it's set for fifteen hours and a few minutes."

"Can't it be defused?" Rylev asked, gradually backing away.

"Not by me. I've read in orders that we keep specialists for this. They're located in strategic cities throughout the republic. We'll have to get a crew here within the next few hours," the young officer said.

The silver object, flecked with blood, stood in the middle of the group, its lights blinking, the liquid crystal display silently ticking off the seconds. It showed a little more than fifteen hours now.

"Try to lift it," Gladkov said. "Maybe we can move it out of town, maybe into the mountains."

"Don't touch it!" the young officer said, his voice an octave higher than usual. "Some of them are booby-trapped."

"I suggest we talk this over in my office," Gladkov said, directing himself to Rylev.

The tall colonel turned on his heel and left the building. At the entrance, he saw his second in command. "Search the whole building for our people," he ordered. "We should have had more guards on duty."

"I have, sir. The two at the back are dead. We lost seven altogether."

"Get them out of here and lay them out in a hangar at the airport. How many casualties so far?"

"Eleven that we know of, sir."

"Damn! Who in hell is responsible for all this?" he said as if talking to himself. "When you've got our people bagged and stored at the airport, I want you to scour this town, every building, every room."

"What about the surrounding country, the hills?" the major asked.

"Report to me after you've searched the town again. I'll be at Colonel Gladkov's office."

Gladkov came out of the building at that time and climbed into his staff car. Rylev climbed in without invitation. They drove to the converted KGB headquarters in silence. The offices in front were undamaged.

Gladkov looked more confident sitting behind his desk than the last time they met.

"We're both in deep shit," Rylev said, slumping in his chair and unbuttoning his fatigues. "What the hell do you suggest?"

"We evacuate," Gladkov said simply.

"I should have known," Rylev snarled. "An easy solution, but one that leaves no alternative but the gulags for us. Jesus! Why me?" he went on, his face a mask of doubt and pain. "This will be the worst blow to Spetsnaz honor since we were formed."

"If you don't want to evacuate, what do you suggest?" Gladkov asked, his hands working nervously on the new leather baton, bending it, sliding fingers along it, slapping it on the desk.

"When my men have made the search, one of your soldiers and one of mine will try to lift it," Rylev said, grasping at any solution. "The rest will be posted a mile from the blast area."

"We might as well be dead if the thing blows," Gladkov

said. "The whole repository would go with it. Do you know what we've got in that building?"

"Don't remind me," Rylev said. "I can't believe Morozov, our glorious leader, could have been so stupid. He's put us in one hell of a fix, Nikolai Ivanovich. We're damned if we do and dead if we don't."

"Shall I tell you what you said when I uttered those words?"

"Don't remind me."

"What about the specialist squads?" Gladkov asked. "Can we get communications to them?"

"We can try to put together something workable from what we have," the Spetsnaz colonel suggested. "My special transmitters have been tampered with, some parts stolen and tossed away. What about you?"

"The whole communications building is gone, a mess of nuts and bolts and wires. Maybe we have a private transmitter somewhere. I'll have my men look for one."

A staff car glided up to Gladkov's headquarters. A major in the service of the Inspector General's Office alighted from the car. He was tall and moved with the grace of a jungle cat. His uniform was immaculate. A sentry at the entrance challenged him. He showed his identification and marched in as if he owned the place. While Carter handled this alone, Nadya, in the uniform of his aide (part of Howard Schmidt's carefully planned gear), stayed at the wheel of the stolen car, her hands tapping nervously on the wheel.

The two colonels were sitting dejectedly in the small office when the new man entered. He marched smartly to the front of the desk and saluted.

"Major Kerensky, sir," he said. "Office of the Inspector General."

"What the hell . . . ? Where did you come from?" Gladkov asked, slapping his baton on the table.

"My plane landed during a series of explosions. No one to meet me. Just what is going on here, sir?"

"What the hell are you doing here?" Gladkov asked, his face a light shade of purple.

"Routine check, Colonel. The general wondered why a crack unit of our Spetsnaz was needed here."

Rylev was sitting hunched over, his head in his hands.

"This is Colonel Rylev?" Carter asked.

"It is," Gladkov answered for him as the defeated colonel looked up for the first time.

"Something's very wrong here," Carter said. "You might as well tell me the whole story. I'll find out anyway."

Rylev looked at Gladkov who nodded. He had put aside his baton. His hands were clasped together under the table where the newly arrived major couldn't see them shake.

Rylev recited the recent events with a voice filled with defeat. "So we have no alternative but to call for a demolitions expert," he concluded.

The major had taken a seat without being asked. He lit a cigarette and blew out the smoke while he regarded the two men seriously as if he were deciding what his general would do about it.

"You're in serious trouble, you know that?" the major asked.

"Don't remind us," Rylev mumbled. "Isn't there any way we can clean it up without . . . ?"

"Perhaps . . ." Carter said to the men who were ready to grasp at straws. "What would happen if we defuse the bomb ourselves and catch the men responsible?" he finally asked.

The two men looked at him as if they could not believe their ears.

"Before I was transferred to my current posting I ran the demolitions school at Odessa."

"Yes?" Gladkov said, starting to sit up in his chair. "Why would you . . . ?"

"I hate my damned job," Carter said, putting some feeling into the act. "I've always wanted to be Spetsnaz."

"I smell a deal here," Rylev said, his tone conspiratorial. "You take care of the bomb. I use my influence to help with a transfer."

"With my recommendation," Gladkov added. He had picked up his baton and was flicking it against his pant leg under the table.

"Suppose I can defuse the bomb. Can you control the enemy?" Carter asked. "The deal isn't worth a damn if you can't."

Rylev kicked the other colonel under the table. "Guaranteed," he said. "You look after the bomb, we take care of the infiltrators. You give us a favorable report in Moscow."

"And you work on my transfer or my report suddenly changes," Carter reminded them, a leer on his handsome face.

Gladkov brought out the vodka, poured three glasses, and handed them around. "To success," he said.

They all drained their glasses.

"What do you need from us?" Rykov asked.

"I don't need personnel. My aide was an instructor at the school. She was one of the best. Has the bomb a timer?" Carter asked.

"Yes. It's set for about fourteen hours," Rylev said.

"I'd better look at it. Then we'll decide," Carter said, putting down his glass and standing before the others.

They drove to the science building, Nadya following the other staff car. When they arrived, they were met by a couple of soldiers.

One of them saluted. "We weren't able to move the object, Colonel. It's too heavy," he said.

"You ordered someone to move it before we arrived?"

Carter said, trying to look as shocked as possible.

"Yes. We ordered an evacuation and had two men try to move it out of here," Rylev said, feeling queasy at the thought. They had not ordered the evacuation. He and Gladkov sat discussing the issue while these two oafs were struggling to move the damned thing.

"That could have had serious consequences, Colonel," Carter said wryly. "How did it get here anyway?"

"We'll discuss that later," Rylev said. "You don't have much time." He glanced at the timer. "You have less than fourteen hours to dismantle the timer."

Carter smiled to himself while keeping a straight face. He knew that Rylev had no intention of letting him and Nadya do their jobs and leave the town alive. If they declared the bomb disarmed, they would be disposed of, the place cleaned up, and some plausible story concocted to save the reputation of the two military leaders.

"Standard operating procedure calls for you and all your men to be evacuated two miles from this sight," he said with authority. "You will evacuate civilians three miles. This looks like it's a relatively low-yield bomb, but if it blows, it will kill anything within a mile, perhaps more."

"How do you know?" Rylev challenged.

"We don't advertise our mistakes, Colonel. Take my word for it."

"How long will it take?" Gladkov asked.

"The bomb gives us almost fourteen hours. We hope we have that long," Carter said with a smile.

"I will get my men out right away," Gladkov said, turning to one of his officers to give the order. "They will take care of the civilian evacuation."

"My men will not be going," Rylev announced.

Carter and Nadya exchanged glances. Carter let it lie for a few seconds before he spoke again. "We know your men are the finest in the country, Colonel. They would stand guard if ordered. But for what? When you returned home it would not be to a hero's welcome but to a court-martial." He paused to let it sink in. "This is a standing order. You must evacuate."

"Very well," Rylev said, trying to sound reluctant. "My men will evacuate for a mile and a half. Will that satisfy the order?"

"I won't tell anyone if you won't, Colonel," Carter said. "Now I really must insist on a quick evacuation. We have a lot of work to do."

"That's it?" Gladkov asked.

"No. Have your men turn on the lights," Carter said.

"The power is cut off," Gladkov answered.

"I can't believe . . ." Carter started to say. "Never mind. A few high-powered battery lamps will do."

The lamps were delivered and some were set up around the bomb. For the next half hour Carter sat with Nadya near the bomb in the center of the first floor waiting for the town to clear out completely. The man from AXE dragged on a Russian cigarette and sipped at a small cup of vodka. Nadya had found a bottle and some paper cups in the guardroom.

Every ten minutes one of them checked outside. The evacuation was going slowly. Carter didn't want to put his plan into effect until they had the place all to themselves.

"You might as well tell me the plan, Nick," Nadya said. "We've only got a few minutes before we go to work."

"You said something in your apartment a few days ago," he began, flicking ash on the floor. "You were kidding about all the ways to destroy the tapes."

"I can't remember what I said."

"You said we could build a giant electromagnet and degauss them."

"But I said that as a joke . . ."

"That's because you're into sophisticated stuff," Carter

said, grinning. "Think electrical theory. Try this on for size."

He refilled his cup, made himself more comfortable with his back against the fake bomb, and started with his first thoughts. "It made sense when I first saw inside this building. The tapes are all on the first floor. The outer aisles are covered with wallboard, making a wide aisle around the whole outer perimeter. To put it another way, as we sit here in the middle of it, the whole floor is surrounded by an insulated wall and the tapes are inside the shield it creates."

"I get it!" Nadya said excitedly. "Electromagnet! Degauss the tapes. If we could use the insulated wall as the outer shell of a giant electromagnet, we could clean the tapes in no time at all!" She laughed out loud at the cleverness of the idea.

"Suppose I told you that the sixth-floor storage area contained three reels of heavy-gauge copper wire," Carter added. "It also stores two high-voltage gasoline generators and plenty of fuel."

"Yes, yes!" Nadya said, as thrilled as a child with a new toy. "We wrap the wire around the perimeter wall and turn on the juice. One big electromagnet. Wow!"

They sat, grinning at each other, until Nadya posed a question. "How are we going to string the wire? The rolls must weigh a ton."

"Two forklift trucks on the sixth floor and a large freight elevator," Carter explained. "We roll the copper reels on the forklift, then rig it to play out the wire as you back around the inside of the perimeter. When you're finished, you have the whole place wrapped like a Christmas present."

"It should work. But can we handle it alone?"

"I wish we had help, but we've got to do it ourselves," Carter said.

Nadya sat, growing more excited by the minute. "I like it," she announced. "I can drive the forklift, but won't it take hours?"

"We'll take turns with the forklift," Carter said, lighting another cigarette from the butt of the first. "You're right. It will take us hours to string the wire. That's why we had to get everyone far away from here."

FIFTEEN

It was almost midnight by the time the military had effected the evacuation and Carter was able to get the plan under way.

Nadya had been restless during the waiting time and searched the sixth-floor storeroom for ideas on how to get the heavy reels set up to deliver the copper wire.

"Any ideas on how to start?" Carter asked her before going to work.

"It's going to be a long night," she said. "I found a shaft and a couple of yokes that are the right size. I'll need some help."

"No problem. What can I do?" Carter asked.

"Getting the reels set up on the forklift will be the worst part," Nadya said. "We roll a reel on the two blades, stick the shaft through the center core, and use the forklift to raise it to sit on the yoke."

"But the reel won't do us any good sitting on a stationary yoke," Carter said.

"That's just the first step," Nadya explained, almost losing her patience. "I'm doing the best I can." She was close to tears.

Carter knew it had to be frustrating for her. "What comes after that?" he asked gently.

"I found some welding equipment. I burn the uprights off the second set of yokes and weld them to the blades of the forklift."

"Great! We'll end up with each blade of the forklift having an upright piece of steel attached, one that looks like a tuning fork."

"That's it. I move the forklift to the stationary yoke, place the welded yoke under the shaft, and raise the reel so it's on the forklift's yoke."

"That should do it," Carter said. "You secure one end of the copper wire to a stationary point on the steel wall and roll the forklift backward around the perimeter. The wire rolls off the reel until you have a giant coil around the whole building."

"You make it sound easy," Nadya sighed. She was showing signs of fatigue. "Maybe you should ride the forklift with me and guide the wire. I want an even feed so that the finished coil is one long electrical field without the wire touching at any point."

"But it doesn't really matter, does it?" Carter asked.

"It matters to me. If we let the wire run off without a guide, it'll all run together, overlap and all that. What kind of a force field are you going to get then? It's going to be done right," she insisted.

"Welding, force fields, engineering the yolks, driving the forklift—is there no end to your talents?" he teased.

"You'll find out even more about my talents when you get me far away from here," she cooed, smiling for the first time in hours.

It took until two o'clock to get the welding done and the forklift fitted for the reel. They were short-tempered, sweating and bone-weary. But they still had most of the night ahead of them. They backed the rig to the freight elevator. The forklift and the reel didn't fit: it was all too big for the elevator. They had to dismantle it and take the parts down separately.

"We've got to go through this three times!" Nadya moaned in exhaustion. When they finally wired the free end of the copper to the steel core and prepared to roll, it was after three.

At first, Nadya drove the forklift backward, with Carter guiding the copper to the bottom of the steel wall using a long, forked pole, but she wasn't strong enough for the job. She kept driving the forklift into the wall, letting the roll run free and tangle the wire. Finally Carter drove and Nadya fed the wire.

At five, they changed to the second reel and Nayda's nerves screamed for a rest. She walked to the front door for air. She was filthy and her clothes were soaked. She had discarded her tunic and hat. Her hair, cropped short for her new role, was a mess, matted with sweat.

The night was cool. She shivered as fresh night air hit her damp shirt. She stood against the doorjamb, smoking, thinking about her new life and what it would be like.

"The colonel wants to know how it's going," a voice behind her said.

She jumped, the cigarette falling to roll to the ground. "Who the hell are you?" she barked.

He was very young, a private, obviously nervous.

"What are you doing here?" she added as she ground out the butt with her heel.

"I was sent to see how you are progressing. Well, what's taking so long?" he demanded.

He had to be the youngest one the local colonel had on staff, she thought. They had sent the most expendable. She guessed he was probably intimidated by officers and a bit gullible as well.

"It's a long process, Private," she said, squeezing his

shoulder. "And very dangerous. Tell them to stay put. If we don't stop the clock soon, the whole thing will blow."

He pushed past her before she could react. "What's this?" he asked, looking at the copper wire.

"Uh, a zero-point atomic force field," she said, thinking fast. "We can't get into the bomb, so we're going to neutralize the plutonium quarks with positive and negative autimatter force fields."

"I don't know anything about such things," the young man admitted, shaking his head. "What shall I tell the colonel?"

"Tell him we need about four more hours. We think it's going to work, but we're not sure," she said. "There's a chance of radiation," she went on. "He shouldn't send anyone else down here. Okay?"

"What shall I tell him about the . . . what was it? Force fields?"

"I wouldn't even mention that. Just tell him we're doing our best. We just need a few more hours."

He wandered off up the slope toward the north end of town and the hills. She watched him go. She was sweating more than ever by the time he was out of sight. What would happen if he told them about the copper? Would any of them figure it out?

Nadya went back inside. Carter had just switched to the second reel and had spliced it to the first. He was sitting not far from the door having a smoke. She told him about the young soldier.

"So he went back thinking we're doing our best and we need time?" Carter asked. "Do you think they'll be happy with that?"

"If he doesn't tell them about the copper wire," she said. "What are we going to do?"

"We finish this roll and skip the third. Just pray that two

rolls'll do it," Carter grunted, climbing into the forklift's seat.

"What can I do while you're laying down the wire?" Nadya asked.

"We've got to escape by sea," Carter said. "It could be this morning or it could be tomorrow. It all depends on whether this idea works," he said. "Why don't you take a walk down to the harbor? Let me know if they have a fast patrol boat we can steal. If you find one, memorize everything you see on it. Go aboard and look over the controls so you can describe it all to me."

"What if I meet someone?"

"You won't. Keep to the shadows so they can't pick you up in their glasses if they're watching the town."

"But what if I do?" she insisted.

"You silence them, quietly," he said, handing her a commando knife.

North of Sukhumi, in a house taken over by Gladkov and Rylev to wait out the twelve-hour ordeal, the two colonels sat in battered old chairs. They had nothing left to say to each other. The one bottle of vodka Gladkov had thought to bring along was long gone.

"The scout we sent out is back," an officer announced, showing in the young soldier.

Rylev sat up, all business. "What did you see, comrade. Quick. Out with it."

"He's one of mine. Keep out of it, Colonel," Gladkov ordered.

The youth stood in front of the two men. He had never been in the same room with a colonel before. Two of them turned his tongue to jelly. "I saw the woman, the assistant," he said, shaking, almost stuttering in his haste to get it over with. "She looked tired. They are working hard. She said they need more time."

"More time! More time! We sit here like jackasses while they need more time!" Rylev complained.

"Knock it off, Rylev," Gladkov snapped. "Your people blew it. We'd be better off dreaming up a story for Moscow."

"What are you doing here listening like a spy, soldier?" Rylev roared at the young man. "Get the hell out of here!"

When the young man had gone, his rubbery legs taking him as far from the colonels as they could, the two men sat glaring at each other.

"Why would a major in the Inspector General's Office have a woman assistant?" Rylev asked.

"Why not?"

"Have you ever seen a woman who taught at a demolition school?" the Spetsnaz colonel continued, voicing his suspicions.

"Who saw his plane arrive? Maybe we have been fools," Gladkov added. They were back in their natural element, suspicious of everything and everyone.

"Why did their plane drop them and leave so fast? If we can't find someone who saw them land, we have to find out ourselves who these bomb experts really are."

"But who else could they be?" Gladkov asked.

"They could be the ones we've been seeking," Rylev offered. "They could be destroying the tape reels while we sit here."

"One man and one woman?" Gladkov wondered incredulously.

"I can't believe the two of them could kill my men as they have. No. They must be part of some larger organization," Rylev said.

"Should we hold them while we investigate?" Gladkov asked.

"No. Let's not panic. The bomb does exist. The clock is running. I'm not going down there or sending any of my men unless we come up empty," Rylev said, pulling himself out of the soft chair and stretching. "Let's get busy." He checked his watch. "They've been at it for eight hours. It'll take us a couple of hours to get to the bottom of this. We'll know the answers before their precious twelve hours are up."

The town was still and quiet. Cloud cover hid the half-moon. No streetlights had been installed in the growing seaside town. Until the northerners had arrived, there had been no need of any.

The shapes of buildings looked eerie to Nadya Karpova as she slipped from one building to the next, keeping out of sight. The gun at her side felt as if it weighed twenty pounds as it bounced on her hip. The knife in her belt made shivers run up and down her spine.

The docks smelled of dead fish and rotting garbage. Strange-looking objects bobbed in the murky water. Most of the boats were old, their timbers rotting, barnacles lining their aged hulls. Two boats stood out among the rest. They were steel-hulled, painted white, their superstructures gleaming in the faint light filtering through gray clouds that scudded by overhead.

She walked down the dock to the narrow gangway leading to the deck of the first white ship. Slowly, looking from right to left, she stepped onto the gangway, balancing carefully as she reached out for the rail.

Nadya Karpova stepped aboard.

Using the forklift, Carter rolled the second generator into place, connected the copper wire to the terminals, and filled both tanks with fuel. He was ready now. He pushed the start button on both generators. They exploded into action, their pistons firing, spewing out exhaust in blue clouds.

He adjusted the fuel feed. The revs evened out and the motors ran smoothly as one. He reached for the controls on the two machines and turned them to high in one motion.

Suddenly there was a flash of light and a cloud of black smoke. Somewhere along the wall, the copper wire had blown.

Carter cursed out loud as he shut down the generators and looked for the problem. The smell of burned wire where it had fused with the wall filled the air. One part of the wall, a steel-reinforced corner, had been exposed to the copper wire and had caused it to short out. The section of hallway was filled with smoke that drifted in front of his flashlight. He worked for almost an hour, making sure the fused area was spliced and insulated, then he turned on the generators again.

Both powerful generators hummed their song of power. The current surged through the copper wire. A magnetic field had been accomplished. Carter didn't know how strong it was or whether it would degauss all the reels, but Nadya seemed to think it would work. He hoped to hell she was right.

The man from AXE let the generators run and moved upstairs to the supply and maintenance room. He was looking for something they could leave behind to booby-trap the building so that the power could run as long as possible before the troops could disconnect it. He and Nadya had so little time remaining.

First, he planned to disappear as the bomb expert, but he would mingle with the Spetsnaz to learn if they had been successful. If they had not succeeded, he didn't know what he would do; those tapes *had* to be destroyed.

While his brain was going over the problem, his eyes fell on several tanks of freon. *Freon*. One hell of a lot of it. Computers required a cool environment, and Carter figured there was lots of air-conditioning equipment around that used the refrigerant gas.

Carter found the welding torch that Nadya had used. He muscled the three tanks of freon and the welding tanks onto a dolly and hauled his cargo to the first floor. He was beginning to feel more like a factory hand than a secret agent.

He set the three tanks of freon in a semicircle and positioned the torch toward them. He used a flint starter to get the torch going, adjusted the flame, and taped the torch to point at the valves of the freon.

He remembered Schmidt's lesson of years before. It had been designed to help an agent improvise weapons. "If you burn freon as it leaves its tanks," Schmidt had recited as he demonstrated, "it turns into a poison gas—phosgene gas."

Carter used the knowledge reluctantly. Whenever you set a booby trap, you never knew how many people would die. It was impersonal and it was dirty.

As he left the building, he saw Nadya a hundred yards away keeping to the shadows. She was beside him within minutes, telling him about the two fast boats, their power plants, and their armament. From her accurate description, they sounded like coastal patrol boats with 60mm machine guns on deck mountings. If they had sufficient fuel and ammo, they were in business.

"Nadya, I want you to go back to the boats and find a place to hide. When you see me coming, we'll take off together," he ordered.

"Why can't I come with you now?" she whispered. "I don't want to be alone. I won't know what's going on or if you're ever coming back."

Carter sat her down on a bench in front of an old building across from the Academy. He decided that a little knowledge would calm her fears.

"Here's what's going to happen," he told her. "I change

back into my Spetsnaz uniform and pass the word that we have succeeded. They will come here to look it over. I will infiltrate again to find out how much damage we did. That's why you can't come."

"Why bother? We've done it, haven't we?"

"I'm not sure. We could have done only minor damage."

"But you're taking too many chances. We may not make it." She began to cry. "I gave you the composite reel. I helped you with the magnet. Now you *have* to get me out. *You must get me out!*"

He held her close for a moment or two. "I have to do this," he said gently. "And I'll be back for you. I promise. Find some food, make sure the ships have enough fuel, hole up where they can't find you, and keep an eye on the two boats. I will be back for you later today or tomorrow at the latest."

He held her away from him by the shoulders and looked in those ice-blue eyes. "You'll be all right, Nadya. I'll be back. I want to get out of here too. Okay?"

"Okay," she finally said, wiping her eyes with her sleeve.

He turned from her and pulled on his coat as he headed for their place in the hills.

SIXTEEN

Carter trudged up the gradual slope to the last camp he and Nadya had set up. He changed back into the uniform of a Spetsnaz trooper, rubbed some dirt on his face, and headed up the slope to the evacuated troops.

The surviving Spetsnaz were dejected, sitting around fires smoking and drinking. Morale was very low. Carter sat among them, not saying anything at first, then adroitly starting a whispering campaign, a word dropped in one ear, a suggestion in another.

"I heard that one of our guys had the building in his glasses. Saw them leave . . ."

"I heard that the new bomb squad are really the ones who killed our guys . . ."

"When the hell are we getting out of here? I heard that the bomb people have left . . ."

The camp became alive. Men talked loudly, wanting to know what their officers were going to do about it. A captain heard the talk and, knowing his men, knew exactly what was bothering them.

"And just how do you know they have gone?" he asked.

"We all know," one of them answered. "It is common knowledge."

The captain moved quickly up the hill to the house where the colonels were holding forth. Carter incited a couple of the other soldiers to follow and learn of their fate.

They saw the captain coming. "What have you to report?" Rylev demanded.

Carter, blending in with the other Spetsnaz, could see that the two colonels hadn't fared much better than he. They hadn't been under the physical strain, but the waiting had obviously taken its toll. They were in a foul mood, and looked as if they hadn't slept or shaved for days.

"It is done, Comrade Colonel," the captain said. "We have seen the bomb squad leave."

"Where the hell did they go?" Gladkov demanded. "They were supposed to report to me."

"You will come with us," Rylev said, waving the captain into the car after he had called for an aide and ordering a general resumption of duties.

They drove to Gladkov's office. The atmosphere was spooky. The whole town had been deserted. Carter left the small group he was with and hung around the perimeter.

Rylev ordered the captain to make sure no one entered the Academy building until they had a full squad of his elite troop to lead the way. Carter drifted into the shadows. He wasn't about to be volunteered.

Rylev himself led the survivors of the Spetsnaz force to the Academy. Half of Gladkov's men had been ordered to follow as support. He didn't know what he'd find, but he was prepared for anything. Everything that could go wrong had gone wrong since he'd come to this accursed place.

He pushed in one of the double doors of the Academy, followed by the captain and most of the Spetsnaz. The place was quiet. It smelled odd, as if someone had stored cartons of eggs inside, eggs that had gone bad.

"What's this?" he yelled as he saw the coils of copper wire. "What the hell is this?"

The man next to him began to choke. Some of the men were on their knees. Gladkov's people were pushing in behind, tripping over fallen bodies, their eyes sore, their throats on fire.

"Get out!" Rylev ordered. He fell to his knees. One of his aides, almost as affected as he, pulled him toward the entrance, but they were blocked off by too many others who were on the floor, writhing in pain.

"Smash the windows!" an officer shouted toward the open door. "It's gas! Use your rifles and smash out the glass!"

Gladkov's men unaffected by the gas ran around the grounds outside and smashed the glass in every window. They retreated for a few feet, out of range of the invisible menace. No one seemed willing to go back into the building and the scores of screaming and writhing bodies.

Twenty minutes passed. The surviving junior officers were cautious. They sent in a private who crept cautiously inside. It was quieter. The screaming had stopped.

The soldier returned. He was no more than a boy. "They have stopped moving, sir," he reported. "I don't think the gas is still there."

The officers huddled and decided to give it ten more minutes. When they finally advanced, slowly, they stepped gingerly over the rigid bodies, horrified by the grotesque faces and the contorted limbs.

One man found the welding torch still burning and turned it off. It didn't matter now. The freon gas had been spent. The flame was not creating any new phosgene gas.

One of the men interrupted the officers who were in the huddle again inside the front door. They were Gladkov's men. Rylev's people all seemed to be on the floor at their feet.

"I think I know what the copper wire is for, sir," he said to the nearest officer. "It's a huge magnet. It was probably energized at one time and could have damaged the magnetic tapes in here."

"Jesus!" the officer gasped. He told the others what he'd learned.

"Tear it down!" one of the officers yelled to a group of soldiers standing around, waiting for orders.

The men tore at the copper wire with their gun barrels and commando knives. Several flashes of electricity arced from the copper to the men. Shrieks and the smell of burning flesh filled the air.

"Shut it down!" one of the officers screamed.

The troops raced around the inside of the core, found the generators still humming away, and shut them down. The officers stood around, their brows furrowed, unwilling to issue any other orders.

"Evacuate immediately," one of them finally suggested. "Colonel Gladkov will have to decide what the hell to do with this mess."

Nikolai Ivanovich Gladkov stood outside the Academy building reluctant to go back inside. He had seen the body of Rylev with the others, the domineering Spetsnaz colonel's face distorted in a grimace of pain, his body curled in a fetal position in the last throes of an agonizing death. Gladkov had ordered a detachment to carry the bodies outside for transport to the hangar with the others. He would have a lot to answer for when he finally faced his superiors. Rylev had found his way out. Maybe a gun barrel in his own mouth was the best solution. Maybe. If he just had the courage. . . .

The scientist who had been second to Pivnev appeared at Gladkov's side as ordered.

"What has happened, Comrade Gladkov?" he asked. "Who did this? Is anything damaged?"

"Someone strung copper wire around the core of the building and electrified it," the colonel said, wiping sweat from his grime-streaked face. "Would that damage the magnetic tape?"

"My God!" the man breathed, color draining from his face. "An electromagnet! If it was powerful enough . . ." He reeled, then clutched the colonel's arm. "No! Oh, no! All the tapes could be blank!"

"You must have backup. I'm told you people always have backup."

"We were going to. But the General Secretary ordered the backup to be created when the underground vaults were finished," the man of science said, sitting on the running board of a troop carrier, numb with the realization of what had happened. "We had nowhere to store them in the meantime."

Gladkov sat beside him.

"I've got a few reserve tapes in another building. Not the most important, but they might save our lives," the scientist said.

"How bad is it here?" Gladkov asked.

"Everything. All our developments in science for the last ten years."

"I order you and your people to test the tapes and assess the damage," Gladkov said with authority. "Test all the reels."

The colonel seemed like a new man, more resolute, as if he had solved the problem and was in complete command. He moved away from the scientist and slipped into his old Zil and ordered his driver to take him back to his office.

As the car passed through Red Square and started up Weilun Ulitza, Gladkov was sitting erect and still, calm for the first time in days. They pulled up to KGB headquarters. The middle-aged man opened the door himself. He walked to his office and sat alone. He looked through watery eyes at the pictures on the walls, his days of glory, and the awards he'd earned, all framed in gilt. With eyes that were unfocused and almost glazed, he looked at the riding crop that had been his talisman. He took it in both hands and broke it over a corner of the desk.

The colonel was tired, too depressed to think about a future that could only lead to Lubyanka and, if he lived, to the gulags.

He slipped the awkward Makarov from his holster. He had always hated that big pistol he had been forced to wear. He chambered a round, put the barrel in his mouth, and blew off the top of his head.

Carter sat in an improvised barracks, the object of scores of eyes. He was the only Spetsnaz in Sukhumi. The supposed elite corps had been wiped out. No one was able to explain the series of events that had led to the rape of the town.

Only one officer of senior rank remained. Major Boris Khodsheyev, a career soldier, an old crony of Gladkov's, had inherited the mess. He was a tall, thin man, extremely nervous, always pulling at a Stalin-type mustache. Almost indifferently, he had questioned Carter in a temporary command post he'd set up in the army headquarters building down the street from the KGB headquarters.

"Do you know you are the only surviving Spetsnaz?" he asked. He had a bottle of vodka in front of him. He sipped from a cracked glass from time to time, offering none to the man who stood at attention in front of him. "How do you explain that?"

"Colonel Rylev always insisted that one man remain at

the point of entry, on guard, sir," he lied. "I had to stay at the airport."

"Stupid man, the colonel," Khodsheyev said morosely.

Carter realized the man was drunk. He had heard that Rylev was dead and Gladkov had eaten his gun. This was the last of their officialdom on the scene. The man was obviously aware of his fate and almost at the point of no return himself.

"Sit down, soldier," the cadaverous major said, his words slurred. "There's no one left to talk to. The officers are shitting their pants. The other ranks are all just kids. You look like a real man." He raised his glass in a salute.

"What happened at the Academy building, sir?" Carter asked, playing the role the major had cast for him.

"Dead. Colonel Rylev is dead and so are all his men."

"What about all the tapes we're supposed to guard? I heard they might have been damaged."

The major hiccupped. He took another drink, tried to light a cigarette with a shaking hand, and dropped his lighter on the desk.

Carter lit the cigarette for the Russian and took one for himself.

"Damaged. Yes, damaged," the major went on. "Some kind of magnetic field got to some of them. They're shipping the rest back to Moscow."

"The rest, major? Then they're safe?"

"Some of them. Maybe the best of them," he said, hiccupping again, dropping ash on his already soiled uniform. "Too late for me. Those bastards are better off dead. They left me the senior officer. Do you know what that means, soldier? It means I get all the shit for this," he said, answering his own question.

"We're shipping the rest?" Carter prompted.

"Got a radio working . . . ordered up a transport for the

tapes . . . two passenger planes to get the eggheads back to Moscow."

The man was getting more and more incoherent. The combination of shock and vodka was getting to him. The place was a shambles. No one was really in control. But all that would change with the arrival of the planes. They'd send someone down here to take over. It would be someone with a reputation. A hardnose.

SEVENTEEN

The military used mostly Tupolovs for transport. The freighter was a modified TU-154. It was modified for both side-loading doors and a tail that swung to one side for mass loading. The two passenger aircraft sent for the scientists were Ilyushin IL-62s, camouflaged. They were probably used for hauling troops to and from postings. Carter checked the airport and saw them land before he headed for the Academy building where the scientists seemed to be in charge.

The building was in a state of turmoil. Hundreds of scientists milled about, some testing reels on sophisticated computers, others loading the salvaged tapes in wooden crates that had been shipped down from the Tupolov.

He walked the first floor. No one disturbed the lone Spetsnaz. He was in battle dress complete with all his impressive weapons. They seemed to hold him in awe. He had seen the new commander and his lieutenants. He managed to avoid them.

It was time to take stock. He found a washroom unoccupied and locked himself in a booth. His tunic held the C4 he had salvaged from the cave, but he'd not had time to check what he'd grabbed in a hurry.

His uniform concealed two packages. One held enough C4 to blow the Tupolov out of the sky. It was molded to a timer. The problem with this new setup was not knowing the best time to blow the plane. How long would it take to load and get airborne? He'd have to guess.

The other package was smaller. It contained less C4 and a radio-controlled detonator. A miniature radio receiver was pressed into the puttylike C4. He detached the transmitter and put it in a separate pocket. Again he had problems with this bomb. What was the range of the transmitter? He might have to be very close for it to be effective.

When he had organized his pockets with the two bombs, he used the facilities of the washroom at leisure and marched out purposefully, trying to look like a man with a mission.

He had a mission. In fact he had two.

Several of the packed crates were ready to be wired shut. They sat with their magnetic tape reels packed carefully in shredded paper. Carter set his Kalashnikov aside and started to help the junior troops assigned to closing the crates and lifting them onto a nearby truck.

The young soldiers were impressed to be working with one of the feared Spetsnaz. They were as friendly as a litter of puppies. They worked for more than an hour, the sweat soaking their shirts under the heavy tunics.

"When do we ship out of here?" he asked a veteran sergeant who had been moving from squad to squad, supervising the loading.

"Hell, soldier. You can ship out anytime you like. You'll be a damned hero back home."

"I'll be a dead man and we both know it," Carter said. "I'd like to get to my family before they come for me."

"This load's due out at midnight. Maybe you can hitch a ride."

"Thanks. I might do that," he said, returning to the work.

When they took a smoke break, Carter turned from them, slipped the bomb from his pocket, and set it to blow at two in the morning. If the radio-controlled bomb didn't work, he'd get the plane with the timed blast.

He checked the work crew. They were still smoking, talking to the old sergeant.

He slipped the bomb into a crate, wired it shut, and hauled it onto the truck.

"I think I'll take your advice," he said to the sergeant. "Maybe the pilot will give me a lift."

He waved to the group as he took off. The vaunted Spetsnaz soldier had been a regular guy. He'd done more than one man's work with them for almost two hours. No one volunteered like that anymore.

The hike to the three planes on the tarmac took a half hour. Carter was beginning to get weary. He walked to the big transport. It was half loaded. At eight o'clock, lights shone on it and in it, making it the focal point of the airport.

The pilot stood with the co-pilot near the cockpit ramp, a captain and a lieutenant. They seemed like kids. They both sported wispy mustaches in an effort to look older.

The Spetsnaz warrior in full battle dress was impressive. He marched straight at them, saluted, and stated his case.

"I'm the only survivor of my company, sir," he said to the pilot. "It's hard time for me when I get home. I'd like to see the wife and kids, maybe lay a few women before they come for me. The condemned man has a last request."

"Need a lift," the pilot said without emotion. "Sure. Look her over and pick a spot. She'll be pressurized so you can stretch out anywhere."

"Thanks, Captain. You've just saved my life. I'll pick out a spot and come back later. You're taking off at midnight, I hear."

"So I'm told," the captain said tonelessly. "You'd better be back here on time."

While the captain turned back to his co-pilot, Carter slipped into the hold. He folded several quilted packing cloths to make a pallet next to the bulkhead where they'd already loaded. He planted the bomb at the junction of the bulkhead and the bed he'd made for himself. He covered it with a packing cloth. If the range was not too far and the envelope of the aircraft didn't shield the signal, the plane would spit in half when it blew.

His mind turned back to Nadya. Was she safe and tucked away somewhere near the docks? He hoped she had found the area deserted and was waiting for him as planned.

On the way to the docks Carter tried to keep well away from the center of town. The sky was clear. The moon bathed the land with a pale glow. Two staff cars passed him, their flags waving in the breeze. Major Khodsheyev sat dejectedly in the front car with his surviving officers. The new commander rode alone in the other. It looked like the last mile for Gladkov's officers. The condemned men were heading for the airport and transport to Moscow.

The docks were almost deserted. Some of the locals and transient sailors had drifted back to their homes when the evacuation order was lifted. A few dim lights shone in grimy windows. The stink of dead fish and diesel oil had not changed.

Not many military men were assigned to guard duty. The garrison was spread thin and the docks were not a strategic area.

As he passed, Carter nodded to the occasional foot sol-

dier who patrolled the salt-encrusted slips. His eyes
scanned the ships at anchor for a sign from the woman who
was still hidden nearby.

The two patrol boats still rode at anchor, unattended,
their white superstructures a contrast to the dark scows that
surrounded them. In the light of the moon, a face appeared
above the cowl of one ship. An arm waved. Nadya had
been hiding in the wheelhouse of one of the boats.

Carter walked casually toward the slip where her boat
was anchored. As he passed the hawser at the bow, he
unwound it from the dock cleat. The thick rope slipped into
the slime that washed against the bow.

He walked past the wheelhouse, nodded to her, noted
the broad grin on her face, and headed for the rear hawser.
He slipped it, letting the rope fall into the water.

When the second hawser splashed, Nadya hit the starter
buttons. The twin diesels cranked over, putting a hell of a
strain on the batteries. The motors cranked slowly, groaned
in protest, then roared to life.

Carter flew into action as three of the guards headed
their way, waving and unslinging their rifles. He was up
the gangway in three strides and took over the controls. He
had just thrown the boat into reverse when the windshield
shattered.

Two of the guards, young men from Gladkov's original
force, stood on the dock emptying their Kalashnikovs at
the boat. A third guard raced up the gangway.

Carter left the controls. He caught the first young soldier as he reached the upper deck and before he could bring
his weapon to bear. Slugs from the dock whistled around
his head as the Killmaster swung at the big man in front of
him. His blow caught the AK-47 as it swung on him. It felt
as if every bone in his left hand was broken. He flicked his
right wrist and brought Hugo into play. The guard had lost

his rifle but he had a wicked-looking commando knife in his hand.

He came on like a bull, taking Carter into the bulkhead and almost winding him. But Hugo had been poised. The two men bounced from the resisting steel, one with a surprised look on his face. The Russian was impaled on the long, thin blade.

Carter couldn't waste any time. He retrieved his knife and reached for the automatic rifle that had clattered to the deck. The next two had raced to the gangway and were charging aboard.

The Killmaster brought the AK-47 around. The safety was off and it was set at full auto. With the Russians firing as they ran, he pulled the trigger. The Kalashnikov bucked in his hand. It stitched three rounds against the gunwale beside the gangway and traced a path through the wood of the rail. Before it threw slugs into the night sky, it punched three holes in the tunic of the first man.

The second guard was protected by the body of the first and he just kept coming. Other guards, attracted by the shots, were now running down the dock. Nadya pulled back the throttles just as Carter was about to get a clean shot at the second guard. The two men fell to the deck as the ship churned further out of the slip.

Carter's left hand was still numb. He scrambled to his feet, tried to balance against the pull of the boat as she rode astern, fighting a huge backwash at maximum revs. Nadya was taking her out too fast. The only man who could stop them now was on his feet, waving a knife in his left hand. He lunged at Carter and slashed the Spetsnaz uniform from shoulder to crotch, cutting deep enough to slice skin.

A blood-slick Hugo was in Carter's hand again. The man stood grinning in front of him, confident. As the two men circled, the boat was fifty feet out of the slip and still moving fast. Nadya reversed the throttles, pulled the wheel hard to port, then stopped. Both men reeled with the change of direction.

They came together hard. The commando knife went in up to the hilt. The stiletto buried itself in yielding flesh.

Carter was shocked as the blade of the enemy's knife disappeared. He didn't feel any pain as the man fell away from him, the commando knife still in his hand. It was not covered with blood. The blade had slipped between the Killmaster's arm and his ribs, leaving only a small crease along his chest that had not started to bleed.

Carter was disoriented and dizzy. He fell to his knees as the boat bobbed like a cork in the harbor. He still had a bloody stiletto in his right hand. His left throbbed with pain. He shook his head to clear the cobwebs.

They had to get the hell out of there. He lurched to his feet and joined Nadya at the controls.

"I'm sorry," she sobbed. "I didn't . . . they were all coming so fast . . . I had to do something."

He pushed the throttles to full power, held the woman with his right hand, and swung the wheel hard to port with his left. They were still near enough to the dock to hear small-arms fire whistle too close as they skimmed away, leaving a white wake pointing back at the town.

"You did just fine," he said, crushing her to him, bending to find her lips.

She shivered as she pressed close to him. "I was so afraid," she said as their mouths parted. "The men were starting to drift back. I didn't know if you'd make it."

"It's okay. I'm here now."

"Will we make it?" she asked.

"We're damned well going to try," he said as he released her and guided her hands to the wheel.

She looked back at the dead men on the deck. "Oh, my God! So much death," she whispered.

They were a mile out now and making about thirty

knots. "Do you think you can steer her straight ahead?" Carter asked. "I want to check this tub out."

"I'll try. How do I know I'm going straight?"

"The compass. It's showing three hundred and ten degrees." He pointed to the needle and the reading. "I figure we'll have to hold at about two hundred and seventy to make the Bosporus." He helped her bring the ship around to port about forty degrees and hold her on two-seventy. "Keep it on that line, okay?"

"I'll try."

He stepped out of the wheelhouse. Since the windshield had been shot away, the breeze was no different outside than in. He moved to the rail where one of the Russian soldiers lay. He lifted the body and tossed it overboard, a burial at sea without the words. His left hand hurt and was swollen. He was sure he'd broken a bone or two. On the aft deck he found the second dead soldier and he heaved him over the side as well.

A canvas cover was in place to keep salt spray off the twin 60mms installed on a pedestal at the front of the aft deck. He pulled off the canvas, sat in the swivel seat, cocked both guns, and fired a few rounds to make sure they were in working order.

The boat lurched and came back on course. He realized he'd probably just terrified Nadya. They were about two miles out. Carter checked his watch before going back to the wheelhouse. It was just past one.

The unmistakable sound of a jet climbing for altitude could be heard above the sound of the boat's engines. Carter shaded his eyes from the glare of the moon to the south. He saw the huge shape in the sky coming from the east, almost on a line with their wake.

The cargo plane.

He fumbled in a pocket for the radio transmitter and found it as the huge plane caught up to them. He pulled out the antenna, switched on the transmitter, and when the red light glowed, he pushed the small black button.

The jet had passed over them by the time he'd sent the signal, and it was past them by at least a quarter mile when a red and orange ball blossomed from one side of the fuselage.

The plane split in half before it traveled another quarter mile. It was down to a thousand feet, the two pieces tumbling out of control.

The tail section hit first. The front end, the jets still screaming, seemed to hit the water in a long slide. Then a wing tip caught and she cartwheeled for a half mile.

A second explosion tore the front section apart as she was doing her strange dance. Fuselage and cargo were thrown for hundreds of yards, entering the water in a shower of debris.

Carter ran to the wheelhouse and took the wheel from Nadya. He turned the boat hard to starboard, cut her speed to ten knots, and circled the crash sight in a counterclockwise direction searching for something, anything.

He saw nothing. No heads bobbed on the light chop. No debris floated on the water. Even the life jackets had been trapped as she went down.

"What was that?" Nadya asked, again clinging to him.

"The reason I was late," he said, holding her tight, bringing the boat up to full revs and steering back to the original bearing. "The magnet didn't destroy all the tape reels. They were loaded on a freighter aircraft for shipment back to Moscow."

"Was that the plane?"

"It sure was, Nadya. The reels are now at the bottom of the sea. It's all over."

EIGHTEEN

Colonel Pyotr Omlinsky had been a tyrant all of his adult life. As a junior officer he had requested recruit training so he could vent his considerable rage on the wretched victims of Soviet conscription from their first day in the service. His talent for cruelty and blind discipline had been recognized early in his career. As he had hoped and plotted, he had been picked up by the KGB. In twenty years he had risen to a position of prominence, the hated enforcer who never failed to whip a failed project into line. He was considered incorruptible, unstoppable, and totally merciless. He was a big man, well over six feet, strong and muscular. His body was one of his most prized weapons. He treated it like a temple to be treasured and nurtured.

The officers who had controlled Sukhumi had failed and, typical of Omlinsky's approach, they had been sent home for the harshest discipline. His report to Moscow had been specific. He allowed no room for excuses. An officer in the Union of Soviet Socialist Republics was not allowed a major error. The state would not condone it. Colonel Pyotr Omlinsky would not permit it. He had never failed at anything in his life.

When the boat was reported stolen, Omlinsky rubbed his hands with glee. He radioed the Sevastopol air base and ordered a wide search of the Black Sea. No international boundaries were to be recognized. The capitalist rapists who had attacked Sukhumi were within his grasp. They were to be brought back alive. They were to be his ticket to the Soviet general staff.

The colonel sat in an office he had confiscated from the navy; he reasoned that a force with only two vessels—now down to one—had no use for a base of operations. He was taking his first short break, sitting alone, when his second in command brought the news. The younger man's face was a study in disbelief: he had never delivered such news to his superior before.

"The Tupulov carrying the salvaged tapes has been destroyed," he said, his voice breaking as he uttered the fateful words.

"The freight plane loaded under my orders? The plane my people guarded? Impossible!" Omlinsky said.

"It exploded over the sea. Two explosions. The stolen boat was near the scene."

The colonel sat immobile. His own judgment, his own standard of performance, condemned him. "Does the search group know the location?" he asked bleakly.

"Yes, sir. They are concentrating on that sector," the aide said, his tone solicitous. He knew that his colonel's fate—disgrace and banishment—was also his own.

Carter took the wheel and set the course at 260° to hug the Turkish coast. The explosion would have been picked up on radar. The sector where they were cruising would be known. A search plan would already be in effect with enemy aircraft blanketing the waters of the Black Sea.

The sleek craft left a wide white wake. He could do nothing about that except pray for rough seas, but the disadvantage of rough water was a loss of speed. They were halfway home. The *Ticonderoga*'s people would be up in rescue helicopters to pick them up. It was a race against time.

They were off Kerempe Burnu point, a desolate jutting of Turkish coast, when the first of the Russian choppers spotted them. It was alone, but Carter knew it would radio their position before it made its first pass.

"Take the wheel!" he yelled over the wind to Nadya. "Keep her parallel to the coast."

He raced to the twin 60s, pulled off the cover, and cocked both guns. He sat in the swivel seat, sighted on the incoming chopper, a Soviet gunship, and held until he knew their intention. The boat was eating up the miles. The longer the Russians delayed, the sooner he would be under his own navy's protection.

"You will return to Sukhumi immediately!" the gunship ordered. The command was issued over the speaker in Russian followed by strongly accented English.

Carter held his fire. He didn't move or respond in any way. At thirty knots they needed another hour to come within range of his people. One hour . . .

The helicopter gunship hovered alongside, just out of range, repeating its order. It was an ominous-looking craft, a model Carter didn't recognize. It's weaponry was awesome—four groups of rotary cannon and eight radar-guided missiles.

The boat was bucking an offshore chop that was created by winds sweeping down from the cliffs just a few miles away. Nadya steered away from the chop, taking the ship's sleek bow toward deeper water. It wasn't what Carter wanted but he couldn't communicate with her. He'd rather take his chances in the heavy chop inshore than be caught miles from nowhere.

The gunship came in at high speed. He'd never seen a

chopper attack so fast. It came in on a line with his stern and laid down cannon fire along his port side, throwing spray over the boat and drenching the lone gunner.

Carter held his fire. The boat lurched from side to side as Nadya tried to control her nerves. She settled down by the time the chopper had turned for a second run. This time it came in from the boat's bow, laying a string of cannon explosions along the starboard side.

Two warnings were unusual. They had obviously been told to take the enemy alive. Good. That gave him more time. He knew the Soviet pilot would be able to use his own judgment in the end and they would be finished unless Lady Luck played a hand. Carter believed in luck. She was a grand lady who served those who were her disciples. To be a disciple you had to be a believer. You had to believe you made your own luck, a positive thinker, a winner.

The gunship, totally confident of its power and invulnerability, came alongside again, closer. Carter could see the pilot up front and the navigator behind and slightly above him.

They made their announcement again. Carter stood and cupped his ears, shook his head, waved that he couldn't hear.

They eased in closer, broadside to the boat, and made the announcement again.

Carter sat at the twin 60s, ancient weapons compared to the enemy's. He swiveled on the gunship and opened fire, raking the hovering ship from bow to stern. His guns spewed out small shells at five hundred a minute. In the six-second burst the two guns threw out a hundred shells. Eight sailed past the ship into thin air. Eighteen hit the shell of the craft, missing vital lines and controls. One nicked a rotor blade and one hit the pilot.

Either hit would have been fatal for the ugly gunship. In less than five seconds the rotors, unbalanced by the dam-

age, tore themselves apart, sending the ship in a slow dive
to the waves. The pilot never knew the fate of his ship. The
navigator's mouth was open in a scream all the way down.

Luck had been on Carter's side again. Luck of his own
making. He still had his skin, was breathing and function-
ing. His enemy was vanquished. His kind of luck.

The Killmaster didn't sit and ponder his victory. The
wreckage disappeared in the boat's wake. Carter moved to
the wheelhouse and checked on his companion.

She was deathly pale, holding on to the wheel with
hands that were white, a death grip as she stared straight
ahead.

"We're heading too far out," he shouted over the wind
blasting at them through the shattered windshield. "Put her
closer into shore."

Nadya didn't respond. The nose of the ship pointed
straight out to sea, still not far off course for the Bosporus
but too far from shore for Carter's liking.

He pried her fingers from the wheel and took it himself.
He brought the ship around, pointing toward the shore
again, still thirty miles from the pickup point. He used his
right hand on the wheel, holding her arm with his left
hand, now swollen to twice its size.

Nadya, standing numbly in the orange life jacket she
had donned, was almost in a state of shock.

"You okay?" he asked, pulling her to him.

"I . . . thought it was all over. It isn't . . . is it? . . . They'll
send more, won't they?"

"We'll worry about that if it happens," he said, holding
her, trying to reassure her when he had no confidence they
were out of danger himself.

By his chart he reckoned they were approaching Zon-
guldak, an industrial town.

They had a half hour of peace, cruising parallel to shore
in a light chop. Then two gunships, the twins of the first,

came in like angry hornets. They were not about to issue warnings; they had probably heard the last radio report of the navigator as he went down, the last scream of a man who knew he was already dead.

Carter turned the wheel over to Nadya and raced for the guns. The first rocket missed only because Nadya had fallen and the boat was out of control. When the warhead exploded off their port bow, he could hear her screams over the howl of the wind.

He looked around. The wheel was unattended. She was on the floor of the wheelhouse somewhere and the boat traced a lazy circle in the water. They had to have control; they had to take evasive action. He cursed as he left the guns and made his way forward on an unsteady deck.

When he reached the wheelhouse, the second rocket hit the stern at the waterline. It shattered the whole stern and lifted the boat in a slow-motion arc to land in the water upside down. The boat slid along the waves for a few feet, then began to break apart.

Carter was under water. He had no time to prepare, no time to take a deep breath. While he had trained himself to stay under water for a full four minutes, it was an impossible feat when he'd barely survived the concussion of the rocket blast.

As he maintained his position a few feet below the wreckage, his first thoughts were of Nadya. Had she survived? If she was floating above in that orange jacket, the color that was intended to be her salvation would make her a target for the angry airmen. They had lost two of their own and a valuable aircraft. No one would survive this action if they could help it.

Stewart Freeman was on the line with the secretary of the Navy. David Hawk sat across the desk from him. He could hear only one side of the conversation.

". . . Tell him to keep his men aloft. I don't care how long it's been."

". . . I don't give a shit what your next assignment for the *Ticonderoga* is! You keep that damned hulk exactly where it is until you find our man!"

"Let me talk to him," Hawk said, taking the receiver from his old friend.

"Mr. Secretary, it's David Hawk. We're talking about my best man here. He's just pulled off an espionage coup that will set the Soviets back technologically for ten years. We can't let him float around in the Black Sea without a sustained effort to find him."

"Sorry, David. We've got to pull out the *Ticonderoga* for the new Israeli push into Lebanon."

"Lebanon's been a mess for so long, another two days at this point won't make a difference!" Hawk roared. "I want my man to have at least forty-eight more hours. Then you can send that rusty old tub anywhere you want."

"What makes you think he destroyed the tapes? How do you know he survived?"

"First, because destroying the tapes was his job. And second, he's a survivor and I want him back."

"It's not my decision, Hawk," the secretary replied, his agile brain weighing the priorities. "It was covered at the Cabinet meeting this morning. The *Ticonderoga* goes."

"Listen closely," the AXE chief said into the line. "I'm calling the President in half an hour and he'd better have changed his mind."

He hung up and turned to Freeman with a wicked smile on his face. "I'll bet you a fast hundred that my man gets his forty-eight hours."

The gray light of dawn had gradually brightened. The light chop had grown to steady swells. Carter had remained submerged for a full four minutes at least three times while the gunboats circled. He came up for a breath each time beside a piece of floating debris.

Carter hadn't seen Nadya. He had heard cannon fire and seen the streamers of bubbles in the water. She would have been a sitting duck, an orange beacon for them to fire at.

Now it was all still. The debris rose and fell in the swells, sometimes in his sight and sometimes in a trough where he couldn't see it.

A flash of orange rose on one swell and disappeared. He stroked for it. His throat constricted as he saw the pale face bobbing in the oily water.

Carter reached her after a battle with debris and the waves that wanted to take her away from him. Her face was held above the water by the life jacket. The left side of her neck bled slightly, washed constantly by the water. The cloth had been torn from her right shoulder, and the skin looked raw, but Carter could see no other injuries.

Carter clung to a large piece of debris and held her close. It was too far to swim to shore. He could have made it alone but not with someone in tow. He still felt the effects of the wounds she had tended a few days ago. It seemed like an eternity, but it was only days.

The water was cold. He could feel it drain the strength from him. She was probably suffering from hypothermia. How long could she last? How long could either of them last? he wondered.

Confused thoughts whirled in his tired brain until he lost track of time. His Rolex still worked but he wasn't sure of the day. Spotlights had shone over the water. They were vague and uncertain, probably figments of a tormented mind. If they were real, were they friend or foe? It didn't matter. They hadn't seen him or the woman. He had held on so long he was numb. His left fist was the size of a football, the fingers almost useless. He shoved it under her belt and hung on to a hunk of the boat's hull with his right hand.

Light returned to the world. With eyes blurred by fatigue, he looked at his watch. It read seven or a little after. He couldn't be sure. Was it seven in the morning the day after the missile caught up with them or was it the day after that? Perhaps Nadya was dead. He couldn't let go to feel her pulse. He couldn't feel the expanding of her rib cage or the beat of her heart. His left hand throbbed so much he couldn't feel anything but the pain.

A buzzing in his ears signaled the end. He'd been close to death before, so he knew the signs. His sight was dim, uncertain. He was cold, numb all over. His ears began to hum louder and louder. And, worst of all, he was beginning not to care. He didn't give a damn. The water was friendly, lapping at him, caressing him. Let the water take him. He knew of a thousand worse ways to die.

The buzzing in his ears increased. It was deafening. The swells flattened all around him and his face was awash with spray.

Something dropped from the sky and held him. A face grinned at him, a face surrounded by black rubber. The face smiled.

The face was joined by another and a third. They took Nadya from him and secured her in a sling. His brain functioned long enough to recognize a helicopter rescue stretcher.

"Who won the World Series?" His waterlogged lips managed to form the words.

"I'm a White Sox fan, man. If they don't make the play offs, I don't watch," the face said.

"You're no American," Carter said as he gave himself up to the powerful arms holding him. "White Sox fans are from a different planet."

He had no more strength for talk. He was in friendly hands.

The sky was blue and clear. Gulls flew by, keeping clear of the rotors above. He gave himself up to the swing of the stretcher as he was winched to the hovering aircraft.

NINETEEN

David Hawk sat next to the bed in the private room he'd provided for Nadya Karpova at the exclusive Ikaria Memorial Hospital in Athens.

The woman lay still, covered to her chin by stark white sheets, her face almost as white. She had not moved since the doctors allowed him entry to her room early that morning.

The door opened. A male nurse, obviously a weight lifter, wheeled Carter into the room.

"They still insist on wheeling me in this damned thing," the AXE agent complained.

"How are you, Nick?" Hawk asked. "You were sleeping when I arrived." His presence in Athens was mute testimony to his concern for his premier agent and it was evident on his lined face.

"I'm really all right, sir," Carter protested.

"You took a few bullets early in this one. Your left hand is in a cast. You were half dead when they fished you out," Hawk chided. "And you tell me you're all right?"

The sound of Carter's voice reached the woman's subconscious. Her eyes fluttered. Slowly she came around,

her eyes searching the ceiling, then settling on the rugged
face of the man who'd dropped into her life and accomplished the impossible. The smile that lit her wan face was
like a slowly rising sun. Color came to her cheeks. It was
like watching a rose bloom and change color at the same
time.

"Nick," she whispered. "You're alive." She looked
briefly around the room. "Where are we?"

He wheeled to her bed and sought her hand with his
good one. "I'm alive and kicking, and we're at a private
hospital in Athens. But how about you? How are you feeling?"

"Weak. A crushing headache. But I don't think it's anything serious."

"They tell me you have a slight concussion, Miss Karpova," Hawk said. "You suffered severe shock from the
explosion, but that's dissipating."

She looked at him with a furrowed brow, then to Carter.

"This is David Hawk, my boss," he explained. "He
usually stays in his office in Washington, D.C., pays the
bills, and worries about his people," Carter said. The af-
fection he felt for the man showed in his introduction. "We
must have done something really good to rate a hospital
visit."

"I had to set up a new station chief in Athens," the older
man lied, his hand playing with his cigar case. "And I
wanted to talk to Miss Karpova."

He looked at the dark-haired young woman in the bed,
and he smiled warmly at her. "We are very grateful to you
for your help," he went on. "The transmission of the tape
reel you prepared reached us in excellent condition. Our
best people are already at work on it."

"I'm glad," she managed to say, her voice weak. "It
would have . . . have been all for nothing . . . if the transmission had been lost."

"Not exactly. The entire repository of Soviet advancement has been destroyed thanks to you and Nick."

She looked sad. "It is not easy to see your own country suffer," she said, a tear in her eye. "The men I trusted as a young woman were cloaked in false identities," she continued, her English slightly stilted. "They were monsters playing the role of benefactors. Like all my people, I had no real freedom," she went on, her litany filled with emotion. "Failure, and we all fail at some time, was censured and sometimes punished." She stopped to reach for a tissue and wipe her eyes. "I had to get out. They wanted more and more tools to destroy freedom everywhere. I just had to get out."

"You can write your own ticket now, Miss Karpova," Hawk said. "But first a rest for both of you. Will you still undergo a debriefing if we give you a couple of weeks to recover?"

"She's not about to change her mind now, sir," Carter said.

Nadya nodded, smiling weakly. "I want to breathe your air, Mr. Hawk. I'm not about to change my mind now. I want my work to contribute to freeing people from oppression, not enslaving more."

"I'll leave you now," Hawk said. "Nick will not be expected back for a couple of weeks. We want you both to have time to recover."

"She's in good hands, sir," Carter said, grinning.

A nurse came in to wheel Carter out as Hawk left Nadya's room.

"Does he have to go now?" Nadya asked sadly.

"He should get back to his bed," the nurse said. She was an older woman, a woman who had seen too much suffering.

"But he will comfort me and I him," Nadya insisted. "Come back in an hour. Please?"

The Greek woman hesitated, then a smile warmed her lined face. "I will tell the other nurses. One hour. But don't comfort each other too strenuously," she said, her deep chuckle echoing in the room as she closed the door behind her.

DON'T MISS THE NEXT NEW NICK CARTER SPY THRILLER

THE DEADLY DIVA

When the telephone rang, Carter almost answered it. His German was good enough and he thought he might be able to pass himself off as Zeisman. But abruptly, just as he reached the instrument, the ringing stopped.

Quickly, he ran back inside the hangar. As quietly as possible he rolled the big door up after extinguishing the bench light. Grunting with the exertion, he rolled the Stutz out onto the apron by hand.

Then he was in the plane. He did a quick once-over of the controls with his penlight, set the gun on the number two seat, and fired up.

The engine caught, missed, and caught again, throwing blue exhaust smoke as it picked up revs. In seconds it settled down into the smooth, assured idle of a well-maintained engine.

The packs on the disc brakes squealed lightly as he turned the aircraft and taxied to the end of the apron. At the same time, he turned his head toward the darkness at the edge of the woods.

The Dorsts were running across the clear space beyond the fence as fast as their legs would carry them.

"Run!" Carter exhorted under his breath. "Run faster!"

Then he saw the uniformed Vopo. He was standing at the edge of the woods, shouting, his rifle raised to his shoulder.

The couple passed out of sight behind the gate as the

Vopo fired. Carter grabbed the Beretta and vaulted from the plane. He hit the apron running, and was about twenty feet from the small door when it opened and the Dorsts burst through.

Peter Dorst was half carrying, half dragging his wife as he kicked the door closed. Two slugs slammed into it from the other side. He turned to Carter with tears streaming down his cheeks.

"Ruperta, she's hit."

Carter looked down where the woman's white face peeked from under her husband's arm. There were tears of pain in her eyes, but she was smiling.

"I . . . I think it is my back . . . somewhere."

"Can you get her to the plane?" Carter rasped.

"I think so."

"Then move!"

Carter dropped to one knee. He lifted the makeshift Beretta in both hands to the firing position and waited. Behind him, he could hear the old man's dragging footsteps and his heavy breathing.

The door in the gate slammed open and the Vopo lurched through. All his concentration was on the plane and the fleeing couple. He didn't even see Carter until the Killmaster fired, twice.

Both 9mm slugs hit him center chest. The Vopo dropped his rifle and fell back through the door.

Carter sprinted to the plane.

Dorst was struggling, trying to lift his wife up and through the small door. As gently yet as swiftly as possible, Carter got his arms under her and brought her up and into the rear seat. Then he hefted the old man in behind her.

"You'll have to take care of her yourself. I have to fly."

"I understand."

"Here's a light," Carter said. "There is a first aid kit

there, in the pocket. The main thing is to stop the bleeding."

He slammed the door and scrambled over the console into the number one seat.

He kicked the revs up and released the brakes at the same time. The Stutz lurched forward.

In the distance, coming from the main terminal area across the main runways, he could see a helicopter coming their way in the air and the lights of a heavy vehicle on the ground.

He upped the revs and turned onto the old, rutted taxiway.

Cool, he thought, *be cool.* He kept one eye ahead and one eye on the instruments going through a checklist as he sensed the helicopter's dancing spotlight heading right for the hangar.

The pitch was fine as he ran the power up to 1700 rpm. All the instruments were in normal ranges. Magneto drop was 125 rpm. Carburetor was applying heat, good suction pressure with a normal rpm drop.

He put the prop through a cycle from fine through coarse pitch back to fine, and it sounded gutsy.

The gyros were set and the altimeter read sea level.

He flipped the boost pump to on and gave it ten degrees flap. Out the window he could see the flaps cycling down. He left the navigational and strobe lights off.

With any luck the helicopter and truck wouldn't see him in the darkness, and wouldn't hear him over the roar of their own engines.

Then he saw the truck, Vopos already pouring off its flat bed. There were orange flashes everywhere as they hit the ground and fanned out. A slug hit the Plexiglas and careened away. Another came right on through and slammed into the radio box above Carter's head.

He hit the rudders and swung the little plane in a 180-

degree turn on the runup pad until the nose was aligned to the center line.

"How are we?" he shouted over his shoulder.

"I don't know," Dorst answered. "I think I have stopped the bleeding. She has passed out."

"Well, buckle her up, and yourself," Carter said. "Ten minutes from now and we're home."

He didn't add, *if they don't blow us to hell first*.

He lowered the flaps to their limits and put them back to their trailing position. He fine-pitched the prop, and the Stutz, pinioned by the brakes, seemed to crouch on its nose gear, waiting to leap.

In the side mirror Carter could see the orange flashes getting closer, and he could hear the pings as the slugs slammed into the plane.

He hit the throttle and released the brakes.

Half.

Three-quarters.

Full.

From the cockpit the movement of the center line stripe became a blur and then a solid strip of faded white.

"Seventy knots, seventy-five . . . c'mom, baby!"

And then he saw them, two trucks, twin pairs of headlights coming down the runway straight at them.

There was little doubt as to their intent. If bullets wouldn't stop the little plane, then trucks would. They meant to hit him on each side with the heavy vehicles and rip the slender wings right off the plane's body.

"Dorst . . . ?"

"Yes, I see them."

"Hold your wife steady and do the best you can yourself. I'm going over the grass median to the main runway."

The words were scarcely out of Carter's mouth when his feet hit the rudders. The plane veered right and they were in the pulpy mush of the median.

The tires bogged, but between speed and lift they managed to slog through. Carter bit his lip and held the throttle at full.

He only hoped that there were no drainage ditches. If there were, the plane would nose over, probably flip, and it was all over.

The two trucks had veered with him. Now they were also on the median, but their tremendous weight was bogging them down to a crawl.

At last there was a final bump and they were on the main runway. Again Carter found the center line and in no time he got airspeed.

"One of the trucks is stuck!" Dorst called from the rear seat. "The other is on the runway but falling behind!"

"Good," Carter said, and pulled back on the wheel.

Then they had liftoff and the runway fell away. The landing gear hesitated but eventually lifted up into the belly.

Carter settled the airspeed for a fractional rate of climb, trimmed out the control pressures, and checked his oil.

The heat gauge was popping the red and climbing.

The hell with it, he thought, and didn't bother easing back the rpm. It was a twenty-mile flight. If the engine blew on the way down, then let it blow.

Visibility was nearly unlimited and the air was calm in the cloudless night. Calm except for the banshee whooshing as it came through the hole made by the bullet.

Off to their right was West Berlin. Carter put the Stutz into a rolling bank and nearly collided with the helicopter as it came up from beneath them.

"Jesus . . ."

"Willi, look out!" Dorst wailed.

The side door of the chopper was open. The machine was so close that Carter could make out the shooter's features in the panel lights as he let go with the assault rifle.

The slugs stitched across the Plexiglas, and Carter felt a tug at his right shoulder and then burning pain.

From behind him there was a gargled gasp but he didn't have time to investigate. He put the plane into a roll that it wasn't designed to make, and came up under and behind the helicopter.

The engine was still screaming, but the heat gauge was clear through the red.

Much longer like this and it would lock up.

As Carter had hoped, the helicopter pilot was savvy. He waited until Carter came out of the loop and then took the Killmaster's dare. He dropped in right beside them and tilted his nose forward to match the Stutz's speed. In the open hatchway, Carter could see the second man jamming a new magazine into the rifle.

Keeping the Stutz steady with his knees, Carter opened the vent window. Leaning far back, he held the Beretta out the window in his right hand, with a fresh clip in his left.

The other man was just lifting the rifle when Carter fired until the clip was empty.

He knew he had a hit when the rifle lifted, the orange flashes going harmlessly into the sky.

Carter rammed home the new clip and started firing again. This time he sprayed the slugs all along inside the chopper.

The chopper pilot didn't take two seconds with slugs flying around the inside of his canopy. He veered away and Carter banked enough to head straight for the Wall.

There was machine-gun fire from the turrets lining the Wall, but at two thousand feet they were a skimpy target.

Then they were over. He banked right and headed for the lights of Templehof. He dropped to five hundred feet and started his glide.

Suddenly there was a choking sound from the engine and it started to sputter.

"Hang on, baby," he urged, "two more minutes."

He cut back the throttle and dropped the landing gear. It groaned and clanked but finally dropped into place and locked.

The runway was coming up fast. In the distance Carter could see the red and blue lights of fire trucks heading for the end of the runway. The tower would be alerted that there was a renegade, so there would be no other traffic to contend with.

He was down to final approach, still coming in too low but not wanting to risk any further overheat of the engine.

100 feet.

50 feet.

The Stutz nosed down in a long glide pattern. Carter could see the shadow of descent from the ground lights. He inched forward in the seat, his hips straining against the belt.

The plane touched down and bounced slightly.

And then the overheat hit. There was a grinding sound and the pistons locked slightly. A second later the prop froze, causing a side swerve.

Carter did his best to correct as the wheels banged down again, jarringly. The jolt threw him forward. His head slammed against the Plexiglas, and almost at once he could feel blood running into his eyes.

Now it was all by feel. He could hardly see the end of the runway coming up and the fence beyond. He knew his speed was too great but he had no prop-thrust in reverse to cut it down.

He waited until the last possible minute before he stood on the brakes.

They screamed as the discs locked, and then flames shot out from beneath the plane when the pads wore through and it was steel against steel.

The nose swerved wildly. Carter moved his feet from

the brakes to the rudder. He veered from side to side on the runway, trying to reduce speed.

Then they were off the runway, skidding on the grassy median. The right wingtip hit a light stanchion. The wing buckled, but not before the plane had been spun around.

A tire blew and the left wing hit the ground. Again Carter was head-slammed, this time against the heavy side brace.

The world was going black and foggy. . . .

—From THE DEADLY DIVA
A New Nick Carter Spy Thriller
From Jove in January 1989